JR1

D1679632

JUNIATA COUNTY LIBRARY, INC
498 JEFFERSON STREET
MIFFLINTOWN, PA. 17059

STAMPEDE OUTLAW

If he hadn't stopped a stampede for the Box K folks, Jess Holloway would have stopped a bullet from one of their guns. But Jess hadn't known that when he charged into the sharp-horned herd and turned them aside. He won the boss's gratitude—and a warning. If he showed up again on Box K range, his reward would be a belly full of lead . . .

STAMPEDE OUTLAW

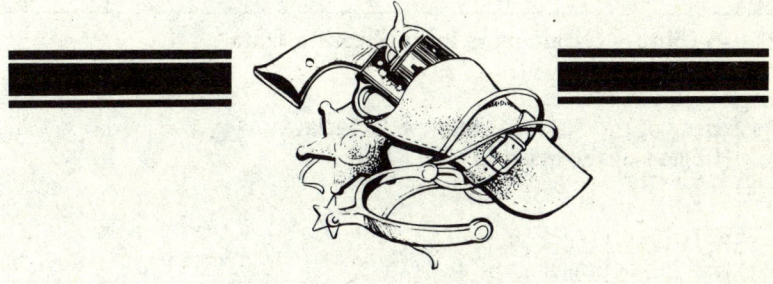

Ray Hogan

ATLANTIC LARGE PRINT
Chivers Press, Bath, England.
Curley Publishing, Inc.,
South Yarmouth, Mass., USA.

Library of Congress Cataloging-in-Publication Data

Hogan, Ray, 1908–
  [Legacy of slash M]
  Stampede outlaw / Ray Hogan.
    p.   cm.—(Atlantic large print)
  'Originally published as Legacy of slash M.'
  'An Atlantic book'—T.p. verso.
  ISBN 0–7927–0058–9 (soft: Lg. print)
  1. Large type books.   I. Title.
  [PS3558.O3473L44   1990]   89–17068
  813'.54—dc20   CIP

British Library Cataloguing in Publication Data

Hogan, Ray *1908–*
  [Legacy of the Slash M] Stampede outlaw.
  I. [Legacy of the Slash M]   II. Title
  813'.54 [F]

  ISBN 0–7451–9634–9
  ISBN 0–7451–9646–2 pbk

This Large Print edition is published by Chivers Press, England, and Curley Publishing, Inc, U.S.A. 1990

Published by arrangement with Donald MacCampbell, Inc

U.K. Hardback ISBN 0 7451 9634 9
U.K. Softback ISBN 0 7451 9646 2
U.S.A. Softback ISBN 0 7927 0058 9

Copyright © 1967 by Ace Books, Inc
Original title: *Legacy of the Slash M*
All rights reserved

STAMPEDE OUTLAW

CHAPTER ONE

Jess Holloway first noticed the dust cloud when he broke out of a dense grove of scrub cedar and started down a slope that led into a brush choked arroyo.

The yellowish pall was neither large nor particularly heavy; it appeared to be moving steadily along the mesa that lay above and beyond a wall of ragged, red colored buttes that faced him from the far end of the sandy wash. It could be cattle—but that explanation somehow failed to satisfy him; a rancher drifting stock to better range would not be pushing them so hard.

But it had been a dry spring, he reckoned, allowing his glance to probe the rolling country, and the soil was powdery, easily stirred. Ranchers would be finding it hard going with the springs dried up and the rivers low. Few things affected cattle raising so vitally as did the lack of water.

He guessed that was one of the reasons Saul Morrel's widow had written him to come; Saul had died, or had been killed—he wasn't sure which, and she had turned to him for help.

He had quit a good foreman's job in Texas to answer the summons, but that didn't bother him—he had been fiddle-footed all his life—he hoped only that he could fulfill the confidence Marie Morrel apparently placed in him. Saul had been like a father during the years they had worked together and he had long sought for a means to show his appreciation. Now, finally, it had come . . .

He looked again at the dust cloud. It had grown, was much nearer, and seemed to be moving directly for the rim of the bluffs towering a hundred feet or so above the floor of the arroyo. Holloway frowned, studied the trail ahead. It did not end at the arroyo's termination, he saw, but continued on, climbing the buttes through a narrow gash that would eventually bring him out on the top. Satisfied, he settled back. Once on the rim he could satisfy his curiosity.

He wondered about Marie Morrel, what sort of woman she was. Her letter had been brief, almost curt, and she hadn't mentioned a son. There had been one—Saul had spoken of him a few times. His name was Dave and at that time he was living with his mother in the East. Saul was working to build a stake and start a ranch of his own. He planned to send for them then.

That time had come six, or perhaps it was seven years ago. Together they were working for the A-Bar spread in Arizona when one spring morning Morrel had turned to Jess and said, simply: 'I'm quitting. Got enough cash now to start ranching.'

Holloway had stared at him in amazement, surprised by the suddenness of it all. But that was the way Saul Morrel did things. 'Glad to hear it,' he said.

'Been a fine thing, knowing you. If you're ever needing a job, ride over to my place . . .'

'Your place?' Jess had echoed. 'Knew you were figuring on one—didn't know you already had it.'

'Got a house, barn, about two hundred head of stock—not much else. Cimarron country of New Mexico.'

'But you've not been gone. How—'

'Had a couple of fellows getting things ready. Been at it quite a spell. Word come yesterday it was all set . . .'

Jess had stepped forward, shaken Saul Morrel's hand. 'Obliged to you for the offer—I'll sure remember it. And I'm turning it right around—you ever need me, just holler.'

That had been the last he had heard or seen of Morrel until he received the letter—a letter that had followed him from Arizona, to New Mexico and finally to Texas. It was two months old when he opened it. Immediately he had dispatched a reply advising Saul's widow that he was on his way, and two days later he was in the saddle.

The Slash M was the Morrel spread, the letter had told him. There were no other details except that he would find the ranch in

New Mexico Territory, south of the Cimarron River. He had been through that part of the country once or twice, recalled now that it was a lush, grassy lowland, broken occasionally by tall buttes and arroyos floored with white sand.

He had camped one night in a grove of cottonwoods near the Cimarron, building a fire of greasewood and creosote bush, and later lain there staring up into a diamond studded velvet sky while coyotes sang in the distance. It had been a night to remember.

But for all its beauty it had then been a troubled country, one where violence rode the hills and mesas as a hard-eyed man known as Clay Allison led a band of small ranchers in rebellion against a powerful land syndicate. He wondered if the matter was still unresolved, if Marie Morrel's need for him had anything to do with the Allison-syndicate war.

He hoped not. He'd had his time fighting range battles and had vowed never to get himself involved again in such a cause. Usually they solved nothing—left only festering sores that sooner or later had to be faced. But if the Morrel problem proved to be of that nature, he would do what was asked of him; he owed it to Saul Morrel.

The arroyo began to narrow, turn shallow. He looked beyond the ears of his roan horse; they were nearing the bluff with the gash that permitted ascent to the crest.

Holloway threw a final glance to the sky above the rim. He was too close now to see the dust cloud, but it had been there only moments before—a low boil floating steadily towards the edge of the buttes.

Abruptly gunshots cracked hollowly through the hot air. Jess paused, reached down to rub the roan's sweaty neck while he listened. A tall, lean, dark haired man well into his twenties, he had deep-set eyes and a thin line for a mouth that gave him a look of firm resolve.

Faint yells reached him, the continuing racket of gun-shots, and a low, drumming sound. Brushing at the beads on his face, he touched the gelding with spurs and urged him up the trail.

He topped out through a patch of feathery Apache plume and glanced ahead. The dust cloud lay a quarter mile or less in front of him, hovered now above a fall in the land. The shooting and yells were below it.

At that moment a small jag of steers, two dozen or so, bobbed suddenly into view over the lip of the swale and raced toward him—and the edge of the bluffs. Two riders came into sight, holding close on the heels of the stock, urging them on with shouts and gunshots.

Amazement, and then anger, surged through Jess Holloway as realization came to him; the two men were deliberately driving the cattle to their death over the rim of the butte.

Waiting no longer, he fumbled in his saddlebags for a bit of cloth, came up with an old undershirt, and then, drawing his six-gun, charged straight at the oncoming herd.

CHAPTER TWO

Holloway, waving the shirt before him and firing his pistol, saw the lead steers slow uncertainly. Immediately the two riders began to yell louder, renewed their efforts to keep the cattle running—straight for Jess and the cliff behind him.

Again anger rushed through Holloway. He twisted half about, snapped a shot at the nearest puncher, dimly visible through the dust. The man veered off, unhurt but visibly startled. His hat fell, and Jess had a glimpse of thick, red hair.

A bullet clicked against his saddlehorn, screamed off into space. Instantly he fired a reply at the second rider—older, darker than the first. He did not flinch and pull away, but calmly leveled his weapon for another try at Jess.

Holloway wheeled then, rode directly into

the thick, swirling dust, offering the man no target. The herd was swinging aside now, beginning to run parallel with the rim of the buttes. Emerging abruptly from the pall, Jess had another quick look at the redhead, bending low from his horse recovering his hat. He jerked himself upright abruptly as Holloway's bullet spurted sand in his face, and jamming spurs to his horse, spun away.

Pistol empty, Jess kept the blue roan moving while he punched out the empty cartridges and reloaded. Ready again, he cut back into the dust, slowed when he saw the two outlaws moving toward him.

He grinned tightly. The pair didn't like his horning in on their little game of slaughter and breaking it up; now they were concentrating on him. He leveled on the dark man, squeezed off a shot. The rider flinched, halted abruptly and clutched at his arm. The redhead gave him a hurried glance, and then both men wheeled and lined out for the distant hills at a hard gallop.

Holloway flung two more shots at them, and settled back on his saddle to again replace the spent bullets in his weapon. Evidently the redhead and his dark friend had no taste for a head-on clash.

He looked toward the cattle. The herd had halted in a small hollow a short distance away, were beginning to settle down and graze on the short grass. Putting the roan into motion, he rode toward the swale, Halfway there, he halted. Two more riders were approaching, coming in from the north.

Holloway studied them for several moments, then continued on. Reaching the dust covered steers, he once again stopped and took note of the brand: Box K—not any of Morrel's stock, he saw, and felt a curious relief at the discovery. Lifting his glance he watched the newcomers draw close. His pistol was still in his hand, and shifting his weight, he slid it back into its holster; but he was still cautious. These could be Box K punchers searching for the cattle—or they could be friends of the redhead—and more trouble.

Both were middle-aged, and one a Mexican dressed in vaquero clothing. He grinned broadly as they circled the herd and drew up in front of Holloway.

'*Muchas gracias, amigo*,' he said, brushing his ornamented hat to the back of his head. 'If you had not come this way, we would have some very dead cows.'

The other puncher nodded. 'Pete's right, mister. Sure obliged to you . . .' He stared off into the direction the outlaws had taken. 'Sure tricked us . . .'

'Who are they?' Holloway asked, easing back on the saddle.

'Call one of them Nemo—other's Red. Ain't never heard no other names.' The puncher paused, motioned to the Mexican.

'Partner here's Pete Gonzales. I'm Ed Floyd.'

Jess nodded. 'Holloway—Jess Holloway. Pleased to know you. That stock yours?'

'Belongs to Tom Lindsey—Box K. We ride for him. Pete and me was drifting them over to the south range. Seen some jasper fooling around another bunch of steers west of here. We rode over to see what the hell was going on—been some rustling lately—and soon's we was out of sight, Red and Nemo must've jumped in behind and stampeded our cattle toward the cliff . . . Where was you?'

Jess waved at the arroyo below the buttes. 'Just happened to be riding this way. Saw the dust and heard shooting. When I got to the top I ran smack into the herd.'

'Mighty lucky for us,' Floyd said, wagging his head. 'Old Tom'd skinned us alive if we'd lost them critters. Eh, Pete?'

'*Seguro*,' the vaquero agreed solemnly. 'He would have been one very mad *hombre*.'

Jess reached for his cigarette makings, tossed the packet to Floyd. 'Things like this happen often around here?'

Gonzales watched his partner fill a small paper trough with tobacco grains, then reached for the sack. '*Si*, it happen too often,' he replied, and began to roll a smoke for himself.

Ed Floyd sucked deeply on his cigarette, exhaled a thin cloud. 'You looking for work? Reckon Tom could use a man—and the way you handled things just now, you sure ain't no greenhorn.'

Holloway shook his head, leaned forward and retrieved his makings from the vaquero. 'Got a job,' he said, building his own smoke. 'On my way to it now.'

'Stranger in these parts?'

'Rode through a couple of times. Recollect hearing about trouble last time I was by—Clay Allison and the people who bought up the Maxwell property . . .'

'Farther west,' Floyd explained. 'Don't bother us none. Good thing—we got our own war going,' he added and glanced at Gonzales.

The Mexican shrugged. Floyd turned again to Jess. 'If you're just riding through, why not take supper with us? Right sure the boss'd like to do something to show his appreciation.'

'Forget it,' Holloway said. 'Just an accident-no man's going to stand by and see cattle slaughtered like that.'

'Honest man wouldn't,' Floyd corrected. 'Where you headed?'

'Morrel's place—the Slash M. His wife—widow—sent for me.'

Jess was instantly aware of the change in the two riders. Ed Floyd frowned, leaned forward slightly. 'You aiming to work for the Slash M?'

'What I figure—leastwise, guess I am.

Won't know much about it until I talk to Mrs. Morrel.'

Gonzales plucked the half smoked cigarette from his lips, flipped it contemptuously to the ground, spat. A stillness settled over Floyd's face.

'Something about that bother you?' Holloway asked quietly.

Floyd dropped his smoke to the ground. 'Obliged to you again,' he said coldly, ignoring the question. 'Reckon Pete and me'd better get back to work.'

Irritation stirred Jess as the chill became more pronounced. 'Which way to Morrel's?' he asked, his manner equally distant.

'North. Just keep riding,' Ed Floyd answered. 'You're on Box K range now, but we'll sort of overlook that. Guess we owe you that much—'

'You don't owe me anything!' Holloway snapped, 'except maybe some explanations.'

The puncher shrugged. 'Best get your explaining done at the Morrels'.'

'Meaning what?'

'Meaning there ain't exactly good feelings between the Lindseys and them.'

'Something I didn't know.'

'Realize that. Big reason why Pete and me ain't running you off Box K range. You're a stranger around here, and you done us a favor. Calls for some understanding on our part—and we're doing just that. Only thing, don't stretch the point. Just move on—'

Jess considered the words, nodded curtly. 'Fair enough—but don't change your mind once I get started. I don't run off easy.'

'Figured that, but don't worry none. We don't go changing our word like some people do. Ain't likely you'll be bothered, but if you do run into some of our boys, tell them Ed Floyd said you could cross. They'll leave you be.'

'Appreciate that,' Jess said, and moved off. 'Hope I can return the favor some day.'

Floyd gave him a cool, level glance. 'Be freezing in hell before I'd let you,' he said and turned away.

CHAPTER THREE

Jess was not aware of the moment when he crossed onto Morrel range. He knew of that only when he came upon a fair sized herd of cattle all bearing the Slash M brand, grazing in a deep swale where a scatter of cottonwoods clustered around a sink hole.

Saul had chosen well, Holloway thought, as he pulled to a halt at the edge of the water and allowed the roan to slake his thirst. The land was rolling with many natural shelters, and was covered with good grass. There was little snakeweed—always a sign of poor country, and while no stream was visible in any direction, green trees here and there indicated the presence of underground springs.

He rode on, wondering how many acres Morrel had claimed and if it were all similar to what he was crossing; if so, his old friend had left a fine ranch to his wife. A fine ranch—and apparently a legacy of trouble, he amended. But he guessed that was to be expected; a man worked hard to get what he wanted, and then harder to hold on to it.

He caught his first glimpse of the Slash M proper an hour later when the road gained a low rise and he looked down into a valley, green with grass and trees. He halted, caught up by the quiet beauty of it.

The main house was long, rambled somewhat as though it had witnessed several additions. Flowers laid bright splashes against its walls and a dense vine of some sort covered most of the north side. Behind it were other buildings—kitchen and dining quarters, the bunkhouse, various sheds, corrals and finally the barn. Again a feeling of admiration passed through him; Saul had done the job up right.

He loped down the slope and passed under the high crossbeam of the gate into which the Slash M brand had been burned, and drew in at the hitchrack fronting the house. Dismounting, he looped the roan's leathers around the shaved pole, and crossing to the door, knocked sharply. Removing his hat, he stepped back.

Somewhere behind the house a woman was singing, the words in Spanish, the tune a lilting border melody. A hammer was ringing against an anvil in the barn, and farther over in the trees a dog was barking frantically at something he had cornered.

There was a sound at the door. Holloway turned, faced a young man. It was like looking at a twenty-year-old version of Saul—the same sandy hair, light eyes, high cheekbones. He had been right—there was a son.

'I'm Holloway,' Jess said. 'Expect you're Dave.'

'I am,' the younger man said in a reserved voice.

Jess waited for him to say more. When it was not forthcoming and Dave made no offer to admit him, Holloway said, 'Your mother home? Got a letter from her—'

Dave Morrel nodded, pushed open the screen door. 'I'll call her,' he said.

Jess stepped into the room—the parlor—evidently. It was crowded with heavy furniture—leather covered chairs, a massive table with carved legs, a large footstool. Framed pictures were on the walls, and above the door leading further into the house was the mounted head of an elk.

Jess paused in the center of the room,

watched Dave disappear into the hallway. He did not mind the resentment in the boy's manner, nor did it surprise him. In Dave's boots he probably would dislike the idea of an outsider being called in to take over the operation of the ranch, too—if that was what Marie Morrel had in mind.

She appeared a moment later, a graying, prim woman of stocky build somewhere in her mid-fifties. She wore a gingham dress and a red checked apron upon which she was wiping her hands. Halting, she looked Jess up and down frankly.

'So you're Holloway,' she murmured.

There was both disapproval and hostility in her tone. Jess felt anger lift within him.

She motioned to one of the chairs. 'Sit down, Holloway.'

Jess moved to an overstuffed leather rocker, stood beside it until Marie had seated herself. As he sat down Dave emerged from the hall, took up a position in the doorway.

'Took you long enough,' the woman said. 'Husband's been dead three months.'

'You sent the letter to Arizona. I'd moved on to Texas,' Jess explained. 'Had to catch up with me.'

Marie Morrel tightened her thin lips. 'Might as well know now—I wasn't in favor of sending for you. Don't think it's necessary. Dave and I can run the ranch.'

Holloway flicked the son with his glance.

'Place the size of this can be a lot of work. Too much for a woman—and a boy.'

'Dave's twenty-one,' she snapped. 'Not a boy any longer. Saul never seemed to realize that.'

Jess opened his mouth, was about to reply that the count of years often meant nothing; that it was ability and the desire to assume responsibility a man must take into consideration, but he let it go unsaid; his welcome was far from cordial without his making it worse.

'It was Saul's wish, just before he died, that I send for you—hire you on as foreman until Dave was able to take over.'

Holloway nodded. 'How did it happen?'

'Gored. He was with the men rounding up strays. His horse stumbled, threw him against a steer. The brute turned on him before he could get out of the way.'

That sounded like Saul, right in the middle of the job, doing the hardest and most dangerous part. He was never one to back off, let someone else take the chances.

'Sorry to hear about it. He was a good man—and my best friend.'

'You should've been his son!' Dave Morrel cut in sarcastically. 'Way he was always yammering about you—how you could handle cattle, and ride and shoot. Got sick of hearing about you, Holloway!'

Jess said nothing. The chore that lay ahead

was not going to be pleasant or easy—that was plain. Dave hated his guts. And Saul's widow resented him. Those were fine conditions under which to work!

'Way I understand it, you want me to be your foreman.'

'My husband wants it—'

'All right, Saul wants me to take over the place—'

'Up to a point. You'll remember that I own the ranch, that I'm the final word on everything.'

'Could make things a bit hard to manage.'

'Up to you. What I want understood is that I own Slash M—that my son Dave is owner, too. Someday soon he'll take over so he's to have something to say about how things are done.'

Jess shook his head. 'Won't work. You can't have three foremen trying to run one ranch.'

'Then don't take the job,' Dave suggested quickly.

Holloway shifted his glance to the boy, studied him quietly. 'Expect that's what you'd like.'

'You can bet on it . . .'

Holloway swore softly to himself. He should get up and walk out right there. He wasn't wanted by Marie Morrel or her son—and he would get damn little cooperation from them in the future; in fact there would be only opposition. Under such conditions running the Slash M would be virtually an impossibility. But Saul had wanted him to take over—apparently had insisted upon it.

He couldn't let Saul down regardless of the problems. They had been friends too long.

He smiled faintly at Dave, placed his attention on Marie. 'I came here hoping I could be of help to you. Wanted to, in fact. It's plain you'd as soon I'd keep riding.'

He paused, waiting for Marie Morrel to comment. She remained silent.

'Well, I can't accommodate you. Saul was my friend—he sent for me and said I was to take over. Maybe it's like getting orders from the grave, but that don't matter. I aim to do what he wants. Up to you to make the best of it!'

Marie shrugged indifferently. Dave said, 'You won't like it here, Holloway. I can promise you that!'

Jess pulled himself upright. 'Try that shoe on the other foot—could be you'll be the one who won't like it—'

'It's my ranch!' Dave shouted, taking a step forward. 'By God—you better remember that!'

'I'll be remembering one thing only,' Holloway said, turning to the door. 'Your pa sent for me. I figure I'll be working for him so I'll do things the way I think he'd want them done.'

He reached the door, laid his fingers on the latch, paused. Looking back, he said, 'Like to be friends with both of you, but if you won't have it, then we'll just make the best of what's left . . .'

Marie Morrel rose, folded her hands together beneath her apron. Her eyes were bright with anger.

'As Dave said, you won't like it around here. My suggestion is to keep going. I'll pay you a month's wages for your trouble. And you'll find a job—plenty of them to be had.'

A perverse smile tugged at Jess Holloway's lips. 'Like this place fine,' he said. 'Where's my quarters?'

She gave him a brief, furious glance and started to turn away. 'Cabin at the end of the bunkhouse,' she said and moved off into the hall.

Jess returned to the yard. Inwardly he was furious at the reception he had experienced but stubbornness would not permit him to back down—that and a deep loyalty to Saul Morrel. The rancher would not have sent for him—knowing both his wife and son opposed the move—if he had lacked good reason.

He pulled free the roan's leathers and started around the house to his quarters. The woman, possibly the cook, had stopped singing, but the blacksmith still worked in his shed, the clanging of his tools a bright, hard sound in the hot stillness.

He reached the yard behind the house, turned left. An old puncher, lean, gray, and with a trailing handlebar mustache and watery eyes, glanced up from the trough where he had halted with his horse. He stared, grinned, said, 'Howdy!'

Jess hesitated. It was the first—and only—show of friendliness he had encountered since arriving at the Slash M. He returned the greeting, started to ask further directions, and then came to sudden attention.

Two men had come from the bunkhouse. They stopped abruptly, hard gaze on him. It was the pair he had driven off at the butte—Nemo and Red.

CHAPTER FOUR

Red hooked his thumbs in his gunbelt as a slow grin spread across his face. Nemo folded his arms across his chest, waited. A strip of white rag encircled the area just below his right elbow where Holloway's bullet had grazed. A third man came from the bunkhouse, a large, thick-shouldered, heavy-featured individual. He paused momentarily, then moved up beside the others.

'What's eating you two?'

Red pointed to Holloway with his chin. 'It's the pilgrim—one that stuck his nose in our business. Looks like Dave's hired him on.'

The big man raked Jess with a cold glance. 'He got a name?'

'Who cares?' Red said softly. 'Going to pleasure me a lot to teach him a few things.'

In the warm hush Holloway eyed the three riders narrowly. The reaction of Ed Floyd and the vaquero, Gonzales, made sense now. He faced the old puncher, watching silently from the water trough.

'They work for the Slash M?'

'Sort of. Redhead's called Red. Little one's—'

'Met them. Who's the other?'

'Walt Zurcher. Kind of heads up the bunch—along with Dave. Special friends of his.'

'Stay out of this, old man!' Zurcher warned suddenly, moving forward.

The old puncher stiffened, glanced frowningly at Jess and then resumed his place at the trough. His weathered face had blanched and hatred burned in his eyes. Jess allowed the roan's reins to drop, squared himself gently to meet Zurcher and the others, pressing in slowly.

'Don't think you're going to like working here, saddlebum,' Zurcher drawled, coming to a halt. 'You want to crawl up on that blue and keep going, reckon we could forget about that long nose of yours . . .'

'Second time I've heard that,' Holloway replied. 'Answer's still no.' He motioned to Nemo and Red. 'They taking orders from you?'

Zurcher nodded. 'Same as everybody else around here.'

'Hadn't heard you were the foreman.'

The big man laughed. 'Maybe I don't wear no sign hanging around my neck, but I sure call the shots—'

'You've called your last one!' Holloway cut in sharply. 'I want you—all of you—off this ranch in ten minutes. And take anybody else who thinks you're running things!'

Walt Zurcher's jaw sagged. Nemo and Red stared. After a long moment Zurcher said, 'How's that?' in a strangled tone.

'You heard it. Get off Slash M range and stay off. I ever find you on the property again, you've got trouble!'

'Mister—you've got it right now!' Zurcher shouted angrily, and lunged.

Jess Holloway, expecting the move, was prepared. He stepped lightly to one side. As Zurcher rushed in, he drove a hard, down sledging blow to the man's jaw. Shocked, Walt went to his knees.

From the tail of his eye, Jess saw Red and Nemo surge forward, crouched, ready to take a hand. He half turned to meet them, relaxed as the old puncher's cracked voice cut through the hush.

'Reckon that'll be close enough,' he said, waggling a Colt in his horny hand. 'This here argument's betwixt Mister Holloway—the new foreman—and Walt.'

Jess threw a glance at the older man, wondering how he could have known his name and purpose; he guessed Saul Morrel had mentioned it. Nemo and the redhead fell back a few steps. Jess swung his attention around to Zurcher, now picking himself up.

The big man shook his head, glared at Holloway. 'You just bought yourself six feet in the graveyard, cowboy,' he snarled, and lunged again.

This time Jess did not pull aside, instead, moved straight into the oncoming man. He threw a stiff left that caught Zurcher flush on the mouth and stalled him, then crossed with a hard right that cracked like a whip when it landed.

Zurcher rocked, howled. The blow would have dropped an ordinary man, but he recovered, rushed in swinging. Jess took two hard smashes to the belly, a third to the jaw—felt himself stumbling backwards. He steadied himself, jerked to one side and drove a hard right to Walt's ear.

Zurcher yelled in pain again, lurched to his left and stumbled into Holloway. Instantly his thick arms wrapped themselves around Jess' waist. Holloway, caught unawares, struggled to break free as Zurcher began to wrestle him about the yard.

Red yelled something and Holloway felt himself being spun around. Zurcher's death-like grip released and, off balance, he started falling. He half-righted himself, then again felt arms encircle his body and he was thrown against Red.

Walt Zurcher shouted, rushed in, fists swinging. Helpless, Jess took a half dozen rock hard blows to the belly and ribs—a solid right to the jaw. His senses reeled and he was vaguely conscious of the old puncher yelling something and moving up beside him.

He saw Zurcher coming in again, but his mind was clearing rapidly. He threw his weight against Red, lifted his leg and caught Walt in the chest with a booted foot. The big man staggered, went to one knee as Red, fighting to regain his balance, tripped and fell, losing his grip on Holloway.

Jess spun, anger roaring through him, and charged Zurcher. As the man came upright, Holloway drove him again to one knee with a hammering flurry of rights and lefts, finished it off with a hard uppercut. Zurcher sagged, gasped for breath, began to sink. As Walt faded, Jess wheeled to face Red.

He nailed the redhead with a sharp blow to the ear, sent him sprawling into the dust.

Ungoverned rage still gripping him, he whirled again, took a long stride toward Nemo. The little gunman fell back, shaking his head.

'I ain't mixing in this. Not my way of doing things.'

Heaving for breath, Holloway halted. He pointed at the pistol hanging at the man's hip.

'That your way?'

Nemo stared, shrugged. 'Maybe—but not now.'

'Then drop that iron on the ground and walk off. Don't fancy a bullet in my back . . .'

Nemo obediently drew his weapon, let it fall to the dust and moved away. The old puncher grinned at Holloway, rubbed nervously at his chin.

'They sort of took me by surprise . . .'

'Keep your eye on him,' Jess said, glancing at Nemo, and then turned back to the others.

Red was sitting up. Zurcher was on hands and knees, head hung low. His mouth was blared open as he sucked hard for breath and a trickle of blood was coming from a corner of his lips.

Holloway stepped to his side, grasped him by the arm and pulled him to his feet. Walt's eyes had a glazed, unseeing look. Jess turned to the redhead.

'Get up!'

Red drew himself stiffly upright.

Holloway, whirling Zurcher around, shoved him at the rider.

'Load him on his horse—and move out!'

Red, holding up the heavier man with difficulty, swore angrily. 'Dave'll have something to say about this!'

'Dave's got nothing to say about it!' Holloway snarled. 'I'm running this outfit—and I don't want you or your kind around!'

'Dave—'

'Forget it! And when your partner comes to—remind him of what I said about staying off Slash M range.'

Red nodded violently. 'I'll tell him—and you can be goddam sure it won't be the end of it!'

Jess, the hard core of anger gone, his heaving lungs back to normal, smiled, shrugged. 'He knows where to find me . . .'

He turned, touched the two riders who were standing on the bunkhouse porch with a look, crossed to where Nemo's gun lay. Picking it up he tossed it to the gunman.

'Now the time?'

Nemo hesitated only a moment, and then shook his head. Jamming the weapon into its holster, he crossed to where Red waited, and taking the dazed Zurcher by his free arm, lent his support to the redhead in getting Walt to his horse.

CHAPTER FIVE

Trusting none of the three men, Jess Holloway stood in the center of the yard, watched them mount up and depart. When they had gone, he turned. The two riders no longer stood on the bunkhouse porch but the old puncher was just behind him.

'By dingies!' the man said in his high voice. 'Saul said you was the kind to get things done. Sure knowed what he was talking about!'

Jess' tall shape relaxed as the last of the harsh tension ebbed from his body, leaving only the dull aches where Walt Zurcher's blows had fallen.

'Sounds like you expected me.'

'Sure did. Saul told me all about you—how you and him used to do things. Figured it was you when I seen you coming around the house. Watching you brace Zurcher and them two sidewinders proved it.'

Holloway moved to where the roan waited patiently, gathered up the leathers. 'You been around here a long time?'

'Since the beginning. Name's Art Gurney . . .'

Jess thrust out his hand, grasped that of the old puncher. 'Remember Saul speaking of you. Guess it was you who got things started for him.'

Gurney nodded. 'Reckon I'm like one of them sheds—a sort of a fixture.' He sobered. 'Expect you know what you're doing—running Walt and them others off the place. Dave and his ma ain't going to like it.'

'Doubt if they're going to much like anything I do . . .'

Gurney chuckled. 'Seems you already done some palavering with Marie and the boy . . .'

'I have,' Jess said and started toward a small house just beyond the crew's quarters. 'You got time I'd like to talk. Some questions I need answered.'

The old puncher bobbed his head happily. 'Yes, sir, Mister Holloway—'

'Jess—'

'Yes, sir—Jess. Be right pleased . . .'

They reached the foreman's cabin. Gurney entered, opened the windows to release the trapped heat while Holloway removed his blanket roll and saddlebags. Stepping into the room moments later, Jess halted, looked around. His quarters contained only a bed, a table with a cracked lamp, and a chair. The floor and walls were bare.

'Seen jails that were more comfortable,' he observed, tossing his gear onto the bed.

Gurney grinned. 'Ain't nobody lived in here for the past two, three year. Saul run things hisself when he was alive. Didn't have no use for a foreman. I'll see if'n the cook can't sort of fix things up a mite.'

Holloway leaned against the wall, drew out his cigarette makings. He offered the packet to Gurney but the man declined.

'Get mine chawin',' he said and dug a plug of dark tobacco from his pocket.

Jess began to roll his smoke. 'Where do Zurcher and the two with him fit?' he asked.

'Dave sort of took up with them about a year ago. Saul never had no use for them—told Dave so. Boy didn't pay him no mind. Always was kind of headstrong and done what he pleased. Always figured Saul was too easy on him. And his ma—'

'Zurcher got a ranch around here?'

Gurney shifted his cud. 'Zurcher? Nope—he ain't got nothing. Just hangs around the Mulehead saloon in town when he ain't up to some devilment.'

'Same go for Red and Nemo?'

'Same. Three of a kind. Sort of wormed their way in with Dave; got him thinking he's big shakes and they're his best friends. They want him running the place so's they'll have it soft.' Gurney hesitated, frowned. 'Recollect you saying you'd met Nemo and Red afore. Where at?'

'On my way here—early this morning. Stopped them from driving some Box K cattle over a cliff,' Jess replied, and related the entire incident.

When he was finished Art Gurney sighed

deeply. 'Sure the way they'd do something, all right. Saul and Tom Lindsey's been on the outs for quite a spell, but shenanigans like that never started 'til Dave began hanging out with Zurcher.'

'What caused the trouble?'

Gurney scrubbed at his chin. 'Take some remembering. Wasn't much, as I recollect. Some little old piddling thing about the range, I think. But you know how a grudge sort of grows, gets worse. Families was once mighty close.'

'And Zurcher's doing his best to keep the fire going.'

'Sure is—and Dave's right in there with him.'

Holloway frowned, flipped his spent cigarette through the open doorway. 'Can't figure Dave. Thought maybe he was just young, trying to show how big he is. Wouldn't think he'd side with Zurcher or anybody else in killing cattle and things like that.'

'He'll go along with whatever Walt tells him he ought to do. Zurcher's got him wrapped around his thumb. My hunch is old Walt figures he can someday own this here spread if he plays his cards—meaning Dave—right.'

Saul must have seen that, too, Jess thought. Such would account for the rancher insisting that Marie hire him on as foreman.

'You know if this is the first time Zurcher tried to stampede Box K cattle over the bluffs?'

'Hard telling. Been a lot of cussedness and pure meanness on both sides. Shooting calves, poisoning water holes, burning line shacks—lot of other things including just plain rustling. Getting so a man can't even get his chores done.'

Holloway crossed to the bed, began to unwrap his belongings. 'Looks like first thing I better do is start patching things up with this Tom Lindsey. Sure can't run a ranch with a war going on.'

'Be natural,' Gurney said, 'only you ain't going to find it that easy. Tom's a mighty contrary critter when he wants to be.'

'I've got an edge—saving that stock for him. Ought to be willing to hear me out.'

'Sure ought. You want me trailing along?'

'Better handle it alone. Got the idea Slash M riders aren't welcome on Box K land.'

'That's for sure, but you—'

'Nobody knows me yet except the one they call Ed Floyd and a vaquero, Peter Gonzales.'

'Ed's Tom Lindsey's foreman—right nice feller. Me and him used to pal around some. Don't know the Mex . . . probably new. Zurcher makes it hard for Tom to keep help.'

Holloway paused, looked squarely at Art Gurney. 'Still not sure about some things. Why do you figure Saul insisted on his wife sending for me? There other problems besides Lindsey and Dave?'

The old puncher leaned back in the chair, cocked his head to one side. 'Weren't because of Tom Lindsey. Saul was the kind who could live another fifty years without even speaking to him if he'd been of a mind. And it was just little things that started between them.

'I figure it's Dave—only thing that makes sense. I think it was because he'd just got this here place built up to where it was a real fine outfit, ready to make big money, and then that dang steer got him.

'He was afraid the whole thing would go down a hole if there wasn't somebody around with sense and guts enough to carry things on the way they ought. He was smart enough to see Dave couldn't do it—and he had Walt Zurcher figured out, too; probably guessed Walt would cheat the boy out of the whole spread before too long . . .

'So he sent for you. Told me a dozen times how the pair of you done your thinking alike—always somehow had the same ideas. Saul had a powerful lot of faith in you, Jess, and last thing he said to me afore he died was that I was to stand by you when you showed up.'

'Obliged to you for that,' Holloway murmured. 'Counting up, I got exactly one friend in the Cimarron country—you.'

'Be more'n just me, come dark. Them two punchers standing on the porch seen you mop up the ground with Walt and Red, and then back Nemo off. Whole crew'll know about it by supper. We all been hoping a day like this'n would come along. Marie hard-mouth you considerable?'

'Made it plain I wasn't wanted—or needed.'

'Well—you'll sort of have to overlook a lot of what she says. She thinks there ain't nothing like her boy, Dave. Except that's how it is with most women.'

'You believe Saul would want me to go ahead and do what I figure's right whether she's for it or not?'

'Know dang well he would!'

'She still owns the place . . .'

'Makes no difference. Kinda like a horse fighting medicine—sometimes you got to force them for their own good.'

Jess Holloway sighed, tossed his empty saddlebags into a corner. 'Way I look at it, too. Just wanted to be sure.' He stared at the smoked chimney with its half moon crack. 'Can think of a lot of things I'd rather do than buck a proud mama and her pride and joy . . .'

'Reckon that's what it amounts to,' Gurney said, standing up to look through the window. 'Here comes Dave—and he's sure foaming at the mouth!'

CHAPTER SIX

Jess settled back against the table. Arms crossed, he waited. Moments later Dave Morrel appeared in the doorway. His face was flushed and his eyes snapped angrily. He gave Art Gurney a hard, passing glare, came into the room and halted in front of Holloway.

'What the hell's this I hear about you firing Walt Zurcher and a couple more of my hired hands?'

'They're fired. Nothing else to it,' Jess replied coolly.

'You're hiring them back—'

Holloway shook his head. 'No. And if I find any more of their kind around—I'll get rid of them, too.'

Dave's face whitened. 'Their kind? What's that mean?'

'Saloon bums—tramps. None of them ever turned a day's work in his life.'

'Been doing all right up to now.'

'At what? Running Box K cattle over bluffs?'

Morrel stared. 'What was that?'

'You heard me—and there'll be no men like that working on the Slash M, long as I'm running it.' Jess paused, looked more closely at Dave. 'You trying to say you didn't know about it?'

Morrel shrugged. 'I've been looking after this place. I know what my men do.'

'Figured you did,' Holloway said. 'Could be you were one of the two who suckered the Box K boys off while Red and Nemo got the stock to running. You and Zurcher, maybe . . .'

'Anything they done was for the good of the ranch—'

'You know better than that,' Jess said in disgust. 'That kind of neighbor-sniping never settled anything—just made things worse and kept a feud going. I aim to put a stop to it—'

'You keep out of it! Not your business—'

'Sure as hell is my business—when it affects the ranch! No place makes any money when it's all riled up and hunting trouble.'

'Lindsey's as much at fault as we are!' Dave flared.

'Could be—but that's not the point. It's hurting Slash M—same as it is the Box K. Your pa realized that, and was probably going to do something about it when that steer gored him. He was too smart to stomp his own toes. And it's going to get worse unless we get rid of the Walt Zurchers and come to an understanding with Tom Lindsey.'

'How you figure to do that? Lindsey won't talk to you.'

'I sure aim to try . . .'

Dave wheeled impatiently, moved to the door. 'You'll be wasting your time. Anyway, who says you're right? Who says we want things patched up with him?'

'I say it,' Holloway replied bluntly.

'We don't need Lindsey—just in the way. Sooner he realizes that and sells out, better things will be.'

Jess studied Morrel thoughtfully. 'So that's the way it is. Whose idea—yours or Zurcher's?'

Dave flushed angrily. 'Mine!'

'Maybe,' Holloway said softly. 'Makes no difference . . . forget it.'

'I'm still owner of this ranch—running it—'

'Not any more. Better get that straight, Dave.'

'You can't come horsing in here—'

'Wasn't my idea. If you were half the man your pa had been hoping for, I'd not be here now.'

Dave Morrel's eyes snapped as anger surged through him. His lips parted as though he were about to make a scathing reply, and then clamped shut. Abruptly, he wheeled and moved through the doorway.

Gurney pulled his lank shape erect, crossed to the window. He watched Morrel until he had reached the corner of the main house and was lost to view. He turned then to Jess.

'You sure twisted the knife in him that time.'

Holloway shrugged. 'Don't like doing it,

but it's about time somebody made him face up. How far is it to Lindsey's?'

'Close to three hours riding. You going there now?'

'Why not? Sooner I talk to him, sooner things will start easing off.'

Gurney wagged his head. 'Got to side with Dave on that. Misdoubt if Tom'll even listen to you.'

'Got to start somewhere,' Jess said wearily.

'Ain't so sure it's safe. Box K punchers won't be the only ones wanting to take a pot shot at you—there's Zurcher and his crowd. He won't be giving up.'

'His kind never does,' Holloway grunted, moving toward the door. 'Which way?'

'Head southwest. Just keep going—you'll run smack into Lindsey's.'

Jess nodded, crossed to where the roan was tied. He gave the blue a quick appraisal, decided there was no need to change horses; the roan had not traveled far and was still in good condition.

He swung to the saddle, touched the brim of his hat in salute to Gurney, and wheeled about. Marie Morrel appeared suddenly at the corner of the house, was moving toward him. Jess sighed, drew to a halt.

'Here's where I get the other barrel,' he said to Gurney and came down from the saddle.

The widow stopped before him, fixed him

with her angry gaze. 'I've been talking to Dave,' she said, allowing that to explain everything.

Holloway removed his hat, waited for her to continue. She was the one with the problem.

'He tells me you fired Walt Zurcher, along with Red and Nemo—all of them his friends. When he asked you to let them come back, he says you refused.'

'They stay fired,' Holloway said. 'Can't trust men like that. Stop at nothing—and one day they cut your throat.'

'Did you fire them because they were friends of Dave?'

'Had nothing to do with it. Got rid of them because I don't want them around.'

Marie dropped her eyes. 'He tells me you're going to talk to Tom Lindsey.'

'Was on my way when you came up.'

'Can't see that it will do any good.'

'Dave's thinking, too. Guess I'll have to find out for myself.'

'What if I tell you I don't want you to go crawling over there—begging him—'

'I'm not crawling, and I sure don't aim to beg. This is as important to him as it is to us. Just want to iron things out.'

'I can order you not to go!'

'I'll do it anyway, Mrs. Morrel. Got to do what I think is right.'

'And you won't let Dave bring Walt and

the others back?'

'Already answered that. I'm giving word to all the hands that they're to run them off if they ever find them on Slash M range. Shoot, if need be.'

Marie Morrel stiffened. 'That's a bit high-handed.'

'Maybe it is,' Jess replied, a trace of impatience in his tone. Suddenly he was weary of it all—of the bickering, the arguing and stubborn opposition. Hooking one arm on his saddle horn, he leaned forward.

'Lady—you can fire me right now if you've a mind to. I can't stop it. But your husband wanted me to take on this job and do it the best I know how. I'm trying to do just that. What I want to know now is are you going to keep bucking me, or are you going to let me do things my way?'

Marie glanced at Art Gurney, brought her attention back to Holloway. 'Saul wanted you here,' she murmured.

'And for a dang good reason!' Gurney declared. 'Give him his head. Let him do what he figures is needful.'

'I don't need your advice!' she snapped.

'Well, you're getting it anyway,' the old puncher said, tempering the harsh words with a grin. 'Saul done a lot of talking to me about Holloway. Won't be no mistake letting him run things for a spell.'

Marie's expression did not change. Her lips

were a thin, set line as she faced Jess.

'You're doing this without my consent. Want you to understand that, Holloway. But go ahead, if it's what you want.'

'And Zurcher?'

'Hiring and firing is a foreman's job.'

Jess smiled. He had made some progress, won at least one victory, however small. 'Obliged to you, ma'am,' he said. 'If that's all, expect I'd better be on my way.'

Marie Morrel nodded, turned and started for the house. Jess glanced at Art Gurney. The old puncher grinned broadly, lifted his hand.

'So long, boy. Keep your eyes peeled!'

'Do that,' Holloway replied and headed the roan out of the yard.

CHAPTER SEVEN

He reached Tom Lindsey's Box K ranch late in the afternoon. As he pulled to a halt at the edge of the hard packed yard, he allowed his eyes to probe the cluster of well kept buildings, halting finally on the main house.

An elderly man, a woman of like age, and a girl were sitting on the porch. It was near the supper hour and they apparently awaited the cook's summons to the meal. Elsewhere, he could see riders lounging in the shade, apparently also awaiting the clang of the triangle.

Jess gave them swift survey, hopeful of spotting either Ed Floyd or the vaquero, Pete Gonzales. Neither man was present. He would be strictly on his own, without any favorable recommendation. He had kept his eyes open for the foreman and the Mexican rider all the way from Morrel's, planning to ask them for an introduction to the rancher but he had seen only three horsemen during the long journey, and they at considerable distance.

Squaring himself on the saddle, he moved out of the windbreak bordering the yard and walked the roan slowly toward the house. Two or three of the nearby punchers immediately came to life. Tom Lindsey glanced up, his broad, florid face pulled into a frown.

Holloway stopped the blue at the rail, removed his hat and said, 'Evening . . .'

The rancher continued to stare. The girl looked up with interest while the older woman, Lindsey's wife apparently, worked at something she was knitting.

'Evening,' Lindsey replied finally in a gruff voice.

Jess could feel the man's eyes digging into him, taking note of his equipment, of the brand the blue wore on his shoulder. He remained motionless, waiting for an invitation to dismount. It did not come.

'Name's Holloway,' he said. 'Work for the Morrels.'

'Know that,' Lindsey cut in roughly. 'What do you want?'

'Talk . . .'

The rancher shook his head. 'What about? We got nothing to chaw on.'

'I figure there's plenty,' Jess said, his own voice hard-edged. 'Mind if I step down? Been a long ride.'

'Up to you,' Lindsey said indifferently.

Holloway swung from the roan, anchored him to the hitchrack and moved forward to the edge of the porch. From the corner of his eye he saw several Box K riders closing in silently from both sides, their expressions intent, suspicious.

One foot on the step, hat in hand, he faced Tom Lindsey. The rancher was about the same age as would be Saul Morrel he guessed—and much like him: stubborn, proud and probably honest. Mrs. Lindsey appeared younger than Marie Morrel, however, and still showed traces of girlhood beauty. The daughter would be Dave's age—dark, blue-eyed, well shaped.

'Said you knew me—' he began.

'Ed Floyd told me about the cattle. Obliged to you—but the favor don't call for no special treatment. Expect you didn't know what you were doing—and far as I'm concerned, you're just another of the Morrel crowd.'

'Not exactly,' Holloway said coolly. 'I'm working for the Slash M—and I'm not one of the crowd, as you name it. Saul had his wife send for me to take over when he saw he wasn't going to make it. That's what I'm doing.'

Mrs. Lindsey ceased her knitting, dropped her hands in her lap and looked up. She was frowning.

'Still means you're working for Marie Morrel and that son of hers,' the rancher insisted.

'Working for myself—or for Saul, you could say. And first thing I've got in mind to do is straighten out this trouble between you folks and the Slash M.'

'Be a mite hard to undo.'

'Maybe. Don't know what it's all about—and don't much care. From what I've heard, it's a lot of little things that got snowballed into something big—'

'Little things!' Lindsey shouted, hoarse and angry. 'Driving off stock, burning trail grass, shooting calves—you call them little things?'

Holloway shook his head. 'Sure don't. But I expect the Morrels could do some fussing, too. Point is, I'm here to end it—get everybody to forget what's happened so's we can both get down to ranching in peace.'

Lindsey tugged at his mustache. 'Can't be

done. Been too much happen—and I ain't the forgetting kind.'

'Not asking you to forget—just to let things ride and not kick up any more trouble. I'll do the same. Slash M riders will stay in line if your Box K men will.'

'Hogwash!' Lindsey said in a voice filled with disgust. 'How you going to control a bunch of hardcases like's hanging around your place?'

'I can,' Holloway said quietly. 'There'll be no more stampedes—or anything else like that long as I'm running the ranch. You've got my word. I'd like the same guarantee from you.'

'Ain't promising nothing,' Lindsey said flatly. 'Be a waste of breath.' He looked at Jess sharply. 'The Morrels know you're here?'

Holloway nodded.

'They send you?'

'Was my idea.'

'But they wasn't for it—I'm betting. Not them two.'

'Makes no difference whether they were or not.'

'Hell it don't! They own the outfit, don't they? Anything you say, they can back off from—and that's what they'll do. I know the Morrels. They're not—'

'Saul Morrel was the best man I ever met—or knew,' Holloway broke in curtly. 'I won't stand for any man talking against him. His being dead don't change that.'

Lindsey's gaze fell. After a moment, he said, 'Was sorry to hear about Saul dying. Real sorry. We used to be good friends, but that woman of his—and the boy . . .'

'Your trouble start with Saul or them?'

Lindsey shifted on his chair. 'Saul. Couple year ago, more or less.'

'Whole thing died with Saul then. Not much sense carrying it on.'

'Nothing's changed. Dave's just like his pa—bullheaded.'

'Seems to be plentiful on both sides,' Holloway said. 'Fact is, the Morrels will meet you halfway if you'll give them a chance.'

'Marie say that?'

'No—not in plain words, but she'll come around once you make a move. Dave, too.'

'Mite hard to believe that,' the rancher murmured. 'And I been fooled before. Ain't about to lay myself open again.'

The iron triangle clanged, sent its ringing call echoing through the closing darkness. No one moved.

'What you want me to do?' Lindsey asked, his manner impatient.

'Nothing special,' Jess replied, feeling a stir of hope. 'Call a truce—a halt on whatever you and your riders have been doing. I'll do the same with the Slash M crew. We'll all settle down and get some ranching done.'

Lindsey considered for a moment, then pulled himself stiffly to his feet. 'Expect I'd better study on that. Supposing you drop back in a week or two—after the drive's over.'

'Was me who made the first move,' Jess said, his hopes dying quickly and a quiet stubbornness taking over. 'Only right you come to the Morrel place if you want to talk more about it.'

Lindsey stared at him in amazement. 'Ride across Slash M range—get my head shot off! You think I'm a damn fool?'

'I took a chance crossing Box K land,' Holloway said. 'If I can trust your word, you can trust mine.'

'Well—I ain't ready to do that yet,' Lindsey said and wheeled abruptly for the door.

Jess watched the rancher jerk open the screened panel and stamp into the room. Mrs. Lindsey rose slowly, smiled apologetically.

'My husband forgot his manners, Mr. Holloway. You'll take supper with us?'

Jess shook his head. 'Thank you, but I reckon I'd better be getting back to the ranch—long ride.'

The woman took an impulsive step closer to the edge of the porch. 'Don't judge Tom too hard. He and Saul were like brothers until the trouble came between them. I think he's more hurt than anything.'

Holloway nodded. 'Yes'm—that and maybe a lot of pride. Like for him to see things my way. Be foolish to let matters run out, get out of hand.'

The rancher's wife straightened slightly. 'Tom could be right, you know.'

'There's right on both sides,' Jess said heavily, and ducking his head politely, turned to the roan.

He swung to the saddle, noting the punchers, still quiet and withdrawn, yet scattered about the yard. He favored them with an impersonal glance, moved off into the night.

CHAPTER EIGHT

Burning trail grass . . .

That accusation of Tom Lindsey's somehow lodged in Jess Holloway's mind and would not leave. He pondered its meaning—wished he had pressed the rancher for an explanation.

He wondered, too, if he had accomplished anything of value. Lindsey was bitter—that was evident; but, as he had pointed out, likely the Morrels had reason for bitterness, too. It wouldn't be all one-sided; such misunderstandings never were.

But he did feel better. The first move

toward peace had been made; and Tom Lindsey was a fair man, if gruff. He'd see the futility of carrying on the feud and act accordingly. Just how Marie Morrel would react when he showed up at the Slash M was something else. He grinned wryly, shrugged; he'd cross that creek when he got to it.

His thoughts came to a sudden halt. Somewhere off to his right he had caught the sound of a horse moving, the muted thud of hoofs, the dry scrape of leather against brush. His hand dropped to the pistol at his hip and he glanced hurriedly around. He was in an area of low, brushy hills and shallow arroyos—almost a brake. Buttes loomed up darkly a short distance ahead.

He touched the blue with his spurs, quickened the pace. It was a bad place in which to meet trouble, if that was what lay before him. Abruptly he halted. A rider swung onto the trail, stopped. Again his fingers touched the weapon at his side—and then fell away. It was the girl from the porch at Lindsey's!

'Mr. Holloway?' she called quickly.

'Name's Jess,' he replied, relief turning his voice sharp. 'Could've got yourself shot, sneaking in on me that way.'

'Wasn't sneaking!' she answered indignantly as he kneed the roan up to her. 'Just happened to cut across the badlands, trying to head you off. Wasn't sure where you'd be. I'm Myra Lindsey.'

'The daughter?'

She moved her head. 'The daughter. You make it sound like something bad—'

Holloway stirred. 'No—didn't mean to, anyway. Just that this thing between your folks and the Morrels has got me stumped. Not sure I got anywhere with your pa.' He paused, looked at the girl closely. In the growing moonlight her face was a pale, silver tinted oval. 'You follow me for a reason?'

'Want to talk,' she said frankly.

'About what? The trouble?'

She nodded, then shook her head. 'About Dave—really.'

Understanding came to Jess Holloway. 'There something between you and him?'

'There was until all this started. We'd planned to be married by now.'

'But your folks won't hear of it.'

'Neither would Dave's. And he's changed—he's not like he used to be.'

'Changed—how?'

'Well—he used to be different—interested in cattle raising, in the ranch. We made a lot of plans, and everything was fine. Of course, he and his pa never got on good but that was only because Mr. Morrel was always insisting Dave do everything just right. I figured it would work out, only it didn't . . .'

'You broke up?'

She nodded. 'Dave started hanging around

town, the saloon—seeing those girls—women—'

'Probably happened about the time he took up with Walt Zurcher and his crowd.'

'That's it! Zurcher seems to have a lot of influence with him. More than I have, anyway.'

'Or anybody else, including his ma and pa. But I think that'll end now. Leastwise, I'm hoping so.'

She glanced up at him curiously. 'Why?'

'I fired Zurcher today, along with Nemo and Red—that pair that's always with him. They won't be hanging around the ranch any more.'

Myra's spirits brightened at once. 'That's fine! But they were Dave's friends. Didn't he object?'

'Plenty! Didn't do him any good.'

'And his mother let you do it?' There was still surprise and a thread of doubt in the girl's tone.

'She didn't like it much either. We had a few words but it ended up my way.'

Myra was quiet for a long minute. Then, 'Why didn't you tell my father that?'

Holloway stirred. 'Doubt if anything I did or didn't tell him will change him much until he's ready.'

'Might have made a difference. He's always figured Walt Zurcher was a bad influence on Dave—blamed him for a lot of the things that happened.'

'Probably right. Zurcher wants to keep things stirred up—but he won't be around now to work at it.'

'But Dave can see him in town if he wants to.'

Jess shook his head. 'Something I can't stop. I didn't hire out as a nursemaid—and Dave's a grown man. He'll come to his senses one of these days.'

Myra brushed a lock of hair from her face. 'I hope it won't be too late,' she said in a spiritless voice. 'Thank you for telling me all this. I—I feel better.'

He grinned at her. 'You sound like it. But don't fret too much. Dave'll be all right, and if I can help things along, I'll do it.'

She gave him a quick smile, and murmuring, 'So long,' pulled off into the brush.

Holloway listened to the beat of her horse, until the sound had faded, and then moved on. He glanced ahead to the bluffs. About halfway home, he realized, remembering the trail from the afternoon. Still a long ride before him—and a hungry one! He hoped Art Gurney would remind the cook to hold back some grub . . .

The trail began to lift toward the foot of the buttes. The brush thinned and the narrow path now wound through piles of boulders, whipped back and forth between scrubby trees. Aware of the climb, Jess let the roan slow his pace.

His thoughts again shifted to Tom Lindsey. He wondered if he had approached the rancher in the wrong way. It might have been better to make deeper inquiries, find out just what had caused the rift between the rancher and Saul Morrel, and then work toward that specific problem. Still might be a good idea. He'd ask Art Gurney about it in the morning, see if he couldn't recall—

Jess Holloway brought the gelding to a halt, a sharp warning suddenly turning him wary. He wasn't sure what it had been—knew only that something was not right. And then it came to him . . .

Ambush!

CHAPTER NINE

Holloway heard the quiet swish of a rope cutting through the warm hush. His hand swept down for the gun at his hip, halted short when the noose settled around his waist, clamped his arms tight against his body. He spurred forward, trying to get clear, felt a second loop encircle his shoulders. Abruptly he was jerked from the saddle, fell heavily to the ground.

Stunned, he lay there struggling to collect

his senses. He could neither see nor hear anyone, had no idea who the ambushers might be; it could be Walt Zurcher and his crowd—and there was the possibility that some of Lindsey's Box K riders were involved.

That thought sent a gust of anger rushing through him. If true, Myra Lindsey was part of it. She had purposely intercepted and delayed him, enabled the others to set up their trap. He swore, tried to sit up. The ropes jerked savagely, pulling from opposite directions, cutting deep into his flesh. Gasping with pain, he lay back.

Suddenly he was snapped forward as the riders at the ends of the ropes began to move toward the bluffs. Holloway slewed around sharply, banged his head against a rock. His senses flickered again. Cursing, fighting the two lines, he bounced and scraped against brush and the rocky surface of the trail as he was dragged rapidly along the ground.

Pain slashed at him as a sharp-edged stone gouged into his shoulder; another wave sickened him when an exposed root dug into his side. Furious at his own helplessness, he tried to reach his weapon but his arms were locked tight to his body and his fingers could barely touch the butt of the pistol.

He tried to see who the riders were, failed. They were too far ahead and the darkness and thick brush made it impossible. Behind him he could make out the roan, however, dimly visible in the dust as he followed.

The surface became rougher. Holloway jolted from side to side as he came up against stiff brush and heavier growth. His head struck something, snapped forward in a shower of lights. He felt himself plunge into a ravine, knew searing pain as he was dragged up the opposite bank. Again his head smashed into an unyielding object. His brain wavered.

He fought to retain consciousness, instinctively continued to struggle against the ropes. A dark wall loomed over him. They had reached the buttes, were now moving along the foot of the formation. Pain eased slightly as the surface of the trail became smoother, cushioned with a thick layer of loose dust.

Out of the brush finally, he caught glimpses of the starshot sky, an occasional overhanging cedar. His back and shoulders seemed to be on fire and his head was filled with pain from the countless blows it had taken. But he clung grimly to consciousness. His chance to get free of the taut, imprisoning ropes would come. When it did—he must be ready . . .

Suddenly the night exploded in a flare of light. A terrible rush of pain washed over him as his head came up hard against the cold edge of a rock. He was aware of being thrown to one side with great force, of flopping back, like a fish out of water, and then merciful blackness closed in.

He opened his eyes to intense pain and a peculiar sensation of floating. The ropes still bound him and his arms, pinned to his sides, were numb. As his fogged brain cleared, he looked about. He was suspended in space. Above him was the star-filled sky, below a rock studded arroyo. The free ends of the ropes had been anchored at the opposing rims of the deep wash; he had then been thrown over the edge to hang motionless.

He struggled briefly, gave it up when spasms of fresh pain gripped him, left him breathless. His head sagged forward, relieving some of the strain on his neck muscles. He twisted gently, tried to ease the pressure of the ropes but his weight was his own enemy and he could find no relief.

He listened then for sounds of the men who had trapped him, could hear nothing but the far off hooting of an owl. Likely they had gone, confident that by daylight he would be dead.

Ignoring the agony, he began to thrash desperately, hopeful of jerking loose one of the ropes from its mooring, disregarding the possibility of death or at least serious injury on the rocks below. Even that would be better than slow strangulation.

Nothing gave. His violent activities served

only to draw the ropes tighter and cut more deeply into his body.

His outstretched fingers touched the butt of his pistol, jammed tight in the holster by dirt and bits of twigs, leaves and other trash scooped into it while he was being dragged up the slope.

Hope came to him. If he could manage to draw the weapon, turn it sideways enough to shoot one of the ropes in two, he would be making a start toward freedom. He would also permit himself to slam into the side of the bluff when the remaining rope, unhindered, swung downward.

But it would be better than just hanging there while life was being choked from his body. Maybe—if he was lucky—he could manage to spin about, take the impact feet first and cushion the shock.

He began to work at drawing the pistol. By swinging back and forth, throwing his legs to the side, he finally managed to wrap his fingers around the butt of the weapon, pull it clear. Then with slow, persistent care, fearful of the pistol slipping from his precarious grasp, he placed it in the palm of his hand.

As his grip tightened about the familiar, worn curves of the cedar handles, he heaved a sigh. That much was done.

Cocking the hammer with his thumb, he twisted the heavy weapon about, pointing it at the rope on his left. The position of the gun in his hand was not firm at such an angle, and he realized he stood a good chance of losing his grip when the concussion came—but he had no choice except to try.

Again checking his aim, he pressed off the shot. The gun bucked wildly in his hand. Powder burned his arm and the flash was blinding, but the rope gave. He turned to it, endeavored to see, but his eyes were blanked by yellow light.

He felt the rope give again. His vision cleared. Several strands of the cord had parted. The bullet had sliced through half the rope, set the frayed ends on fire. Now, a little at a time, the remainder of the rope, unable to support his weight, was parting.

Jess glanced to the slope. It would be a thirty foot downward swing at least—and momentum would bring him in hard. Unless he could manage to take it feet first he stood the risk of—

He set himself for the impact. It was too late to worry about it now. Another strand of hemp broke. Another—and abruptly he was soaring through the night. Frantically he jerked himself about, tried to check the spinning. He succeeded only partly, crashed into the slope of the arroyo with sickening force, his left leg bearing the brunt of the collision. Breathing heavily, he lay quietly, waiting for the pain to subside.

With the pull of the opposing rope gone,

there was a slackness around his waist. Bracing himself with his feet, he lifted upwards, further decreasing the tension. Working his arms, he loosened the noose, pushed it by his shoulders and found himself free.

His body tingled as circulation renewed. He stood there for several minutes, enduring the discomfort, and then employing the rope, he drew himself to the rim of the butte. On the crest, and again breathless, he paused to rest and looked around for the roan.

The horse would be nearby, he knew, unless the men who had dropped him over the edge had intentionally led him off. Getting to his feet, he moved down to the trail. The blue was waiting patiently in a pocket of rabbitbrush.

Holloway sighed, climbed onto the saddle. His body was a solid mass of aches, and across his back and shoulders the scratches and cuts accumulated while he was being dragged, burned with sullen fury.

But he was alive and the fire that scourged his skin from without was no fiercer than the anger that flowed within. Someone would pay for that night's work. Either Zurcher or Tom Lindsey . . .

CHAPTER TEN

It was midnight when Jess Holloway finally reached the darkened buildings of Morrel's Slash M and rode onto the hardpack. Numb, so weary he could scarcely stay in the saddle, he crossed to his quarters and halted.

Immediately the door flung open and Art Gurney's lank figure was silhouetted in the rectangle of yellow light.

'Where you been?' the old puncher demanded testily. 'You was gone so long I got to worrying. Was about to start out hunting—'

Words died on Gurney's lips. He came to a full stop beside Jess, lower jaw sagging. 'Gawdamighty, son!' he breathed in an awed tone. 'What in the name of tunket happened to you?'

'Ambushed,' Holloway muttered thickly and swung stiffly from the roan.

Gurley moved up hurriedly, threw his arm about Jess' shoulders to support him. Holloway winced, swore vividly. The old rancher drew back, stared at his shredded shirt.

'Wonder you ain't dead. Fact, ain't hardly decent, you still being alive.'

Jess grinned in spite of himself, started slowly and painfully for the door. Gurney stepped up next to him, and careful where he placed his hands, assisted him into the cabin and onto the bed.

'Now you lay there, quiet like,' the older man said. 'Got some salve over'n my bunk that'll be just the dope for them cuts and gouges. Got something else you need, too—about a half a bottle of rye.'

Holloway muttered his appreciation, groaned as he shifted his face down position on the hard, corn husk mattress. Closing his eyes, he dozed, came awake almost immediately as Gurney's heels rapped hollowly against the door sill. He became aware of the man bending over him, of the cool touch of a bottle being pressed into his hand.

'Pour a speck of that down your throat,' Gurney said. 'Sort of fix you up whilst I heat some water. Got a right smart of cleaning to do on your back afore I dare rub on the medicine.'

The stove in the corner of the room rattled as Gurney set to work building a fire. Jess tipped the neck of the bottle to his lips, took a long drink. The rye was raw, hit bottom like a thunderbolt, leaving him breathless. He groaned, rode out a full minute and then took a second swallow. A warm glow began to spread through him.

He felt Gurney's fingers upon his back, pulling away the shredded cloth. 'Where'd this happen?'

'Close to the buttes,' Holloway replied in a low voice. 'Caught me in the rocks.'

'Sure did work you over some. What's these here red marks—sort of like stripes around your middle?'

Jess clamped his teeth to prevent moaning. 'Rope burns. Dragged me to the top, then threw me over. Woke up dangling over an arroyo. Managed to shoot one of the ropes in two, get back here.'

Gurney swore softly, crossed to the stove and returned. A moment later Holloway felt him brushing gently at the cuts with a wet cloth.

'Know who done it?'

Jess shook his head, took another jolt of the rye. His back and shoulders began to sting and he realized Gurney was now applying the salve.

'Zurcher. Or maybe some of the Box K bunch. Never did get a look at them.'

The old puncher paused. 'What makes you think it could be Lindsey's doings?'

'Only a guess,' Holloway replied, and related the interview with the rancher and the encounter with Myra. 'She could have set me up for the ambush,' he concluded.

Gurney resumed his ministrations. 'Could be . . . but Myra's a mighty fine little gal, howsomever. I misdoubt she had anything to do with it—leastwise, not that she knowed of.

Could've just used her.' He hesitated again. 'Fact is, don't sound like Tom a'tall. Was I guessing, I'd say it'd be Zurcher and his crowd.'

It was natural for the old puncher to think first of Walt Zurcher and his friends, and place the blame on them. His intense hatred had been apparent earlier.

'Don't see Lindsey stooping to killing,' Art continued. 'And his boys wouldn't take it on themselves. He'd have to order them. Nope—I'll lay you odds it was Zurcher, along with Nemo and Red. You got an old shirt I can tear up for bandages? Couple places cut pretty deep.'

Jess pointed to the clothing piled on the table. 'Be something there.'

Between the whiskey and Art Gurney's doctoring, he was beginning to feel better. Moving carefully, he rolled over, sat up. His head swam briefly and he remained quiet, allowed the room to stop whirling. When all was once more normal he faced the old puncher.

'What started this ruckus between Saul and Lindsey? Said yesterday you couldn't remember. Do some more thinking.'

'Did just that,' Gurney said, methodically ripping one of Holloway's undershirts into strips. 'Was a trail drive that set things off.'

'Trail drive?'

'Yep, that was it. See, it's this way. Folks

around here take their beef to the railhead at Springer, about five days going. Happens the Morrels and Lindseys follow the same trail.

'Things went along with no trouble first time, but we learned something; first herd across had the best pickings—plenty of grass. Next man sort of got the leavings. Best grazing was gone—and what grass was left was all tromped and mighty poor.'

'So it got to be a scramble to see who moved his stock first,' Holloway said, nodding.

'Just what happened,' Gurney said, crossing over and beginning to wind a bandage around Jess' shoulder. 'But that weren't the end of it. Some of the hands got to playing cussfire tricks, making the thing even worse. Don't think Saul and Tom Lindsey knew about that in the beginning—and when they finally did, was too late to do anything. So things blew up betwixt them, both of them hollering at the other.'

Gurney paused, picked up another bandage. 'Whole dang mess fit just right for Walt Zurcher when he blew in. He got himself friendly with Dave who argued his pa into hiring on Walt and Red and Nemo. That bunch sure did make it rough for Lindsey. Reckon last year was the worst of all . . . You hungry?'

'Sure am,' Holloway said impatiently.

'Finish what you were saying—'

'Well,' the older man said, returning once more to the table, 'Saul and his crew got off first ahead of Tom. He didn't know about it, but soon's he'd drove his herd through the valley, Dave and Zurcher and them two skunks of his'n, rode back and set fire to the grass. When Lindsey come along a couple days later weren't nothing but ashes everywhere.'

That was what Tom Lindsey had meant when he referred to the trail grass being burned. Jess shook his head. Lindsey had a right to be riled.

'Saul say anything to Dave and Zurcher about it?' he asked, wondering if his old friend had changed any in his usual reaction to such a senseless trick.

'Was fit to be tied!' Gurney said, handing Jess a plate on which were two pieces of thick steak and several buttered biscuits. 'Snuck this from the cook. Cold, but it'll fill your belly.'

Holloway grinned his thanks, began to eat hungrily. After a moment he said, 'Saul must've changed a lot. Man done that a few years ago, he'd have skinned him alive.'

'Maybe, but things ain't the same. Dave sort of made out like it was all sort of a prank, that Walt and him didn't mean for it to get out of hand. His ma took up for him against Saul. Reckon that's what really tore the blanket—Marie stepping into the argument. Saul sure thought a heap of that woman. She could do most anything she wanted with him.'

Holloway was only half listening. His eyes were on the floor as he munched the dry meat and bread. 'That valley,' he said, not looking up, 'there plenty of grass there for both herds?'

'Sure is. More'n enough, was it handled right.'

'Thing to do then is to make the drive together—'

Art Gurney, in the act of taking a drink from the whiskey bottle, glanced at him, startled. 'How's that?'

'Said the way to get around all this grass trouble is for us to make the drives together—combine the herds and all move through the valley at the same time. Be nobody getting to the grass first—and there'd be no chance for somebody like Zurcher, or Dave, to pull a raw stunt way they did last year.'

Gurney was grinning broadly. 'By dangies—that's sure the ticket! Whyn't we think of that afore?' Abruptly he sobered, set the bottle on the table untouched. 'Only thing wrong—never get Tom Lindsey and Marie to string along with the idea.'

'Don't intend to ask Marie—take it on my own shoulders. Lindsey's the one I'll have to convince.'

'Something else. Be like riding on a wagon loaded with gunpowder—throwing the two crews together. Bound to be a pile of trouble.'

'We can keep them apart. When's the drive set to go?'

'Gather's most done now. Think they're figuring on heading out end of the week.'

'Box K's probably ready, too.'

'Prob'ly. And trying to get away first—same as always.'

'Best I see Lindsey—talk him into the idea.'

'Tomorrow—you sure ain't riding back there tonight,' Gurney said bluntly. 'You're needing some shuteye. Shape you're in, you'd not make it to the gate.'

'Mean tomorrow—after I've hunted up Zurcher.'

'You decided he's the one who rousted you around?'

'Know when I talk to him.'

'Then what?' Gurney asked in a quiet, tense way.

'Aim to square up . . .'

CHAPTER ELEVEN

Art Gurney rode with him that next morning—to 'show him the best way to

Willow Creek', the old puncher put it. Holloway had grinned, accepted the man's offer although he disliked the thought of drawing Art into his personal problems.

But Gurney had been insistent and shortly after breakfast, Jess, stiff, sore and aching in every bone and muscle, climbed onto the blue roan, and with Gurney beside him on his little paint, struck out for the settlement.

After the few hours restless sleep he had, he was convinced now the ambush had been the work of Walt Zurcher and his crowd, despite the fact he had no actual proof. Tom Lindsey might employ every means to disrupt the Slash M's operation, but he was not a man who would sink to murder.

It had to be Zurcher. He, alone, stood to spoil the outlaw's plans, and Walt would want him out of the way—permanently. It was that simple. He felt a grimness settle over him as that realization registered fully. But he'd have something to say about it. He'd been up against Walt Zurcher's kind before.

And then a thought came to him: *that's the trouble up here—everybody's walking around with a grudge*. This is different, he told himself. This is a personal thing between Zurcher and me—has nothing to do with the feud. Or did it? Wasn't it all a part, a product of the simmering, about-to-explode war? He was Slash M's foreman—that made him and whatever he did a piece of the whole fabric. If he called out Zurcher, shot him down—

Holloway swore quietly. An arm's length away Art Gurney heard, turned his weathered face to him. 'Them cuts paining you right smart, son?' he asked sympathetically.

Jess nodded, let it go at that. How could he explain to the old puncher his change in attitude, that there was a need for peace, not vengeance—that a deliberately planned shoot-out was not the answer? Art would never understand. But he was not letting Walt Zurcher off entirely. He had to be warned.

'Might be smart to drop in on Doc Peters whilst we're in town,' Gurney said. 'Some of them cuts is a mite deep.'

'Be fine,' Jess replied.

Willow Creek's single street was almost deserted when they rode in. A half dozen horses stood at the hitchrack in front of the Mulehead Saloon. A buckboard was drawn up before Gholson's General Store. They were the only indications of life.

Holloway angled toward the Mulehead, pulled to a stop next to the other horses. He sat there for a long moment staring at the splintered façade of the squat structure and then swung stiffly from the roan.

'Reckon they're inside for sure,' Gurney commented. 'Them's their nags.' He eyed the animals critically. 'Ain't no ropes hanging from Nemo and Red's saddles. Reckon that ought to prove something to you.'

Jess nodded, mounted the step and crossed to the batwing doors, the old puncher only a stride behind him. He paused there, looked over the top of the doors into the interior of the saloon. A moment later he entered.

Stopping a third of the way to the bar he glanced around the room. Zurcher, Nemo, Red, with two men he had never before seen, were sitting at a table in a corner playing cards. They had not looked up, were unaware of his presence.

Immediately Holloway wheeled and crossed to where the men sat. Walt Zurcher's head came up suddenly. Surprise blanked his eyes. Red and Nemo were no less shocked.

'Reckon you sure didn't expect to see him again,' Art Gurney drawled in a dry, bantering tone. 'Well, you better start—'

Jess lifted his hand, silenced the older man. His level glance locked with that of Zurcher. 'You didn't quite get the job done, Walt. Had in mind to settle up with you for trying—but I'm letting it pass.'

Zurcher eased back in his chair. 'What the hell you talking about?'

Holloway's jaw tightened. 'Don't play dumb with me. Giving you a warning—you're finished around here.'

'You telling me to move on?'

'If you figure on staying healthy.'

'You ain't running me off—' Red shouted,

coming half out of his chair.

Holloway reached out quickly. Placing his hand, palm forward, against the redhead's face, he shoved him back down.

'Don't push your luck,' he murmured softly. 'I'm not sure I like what I'm doing.'

Zurcher shook his head. 'You blaming us for that deal last night?'

'What deal?'

The outlaw realized his error, caught himself, stirred uneasily. 'Well, whatever's sticking in your craw . . . could've been somebody else who done it . . .'

'Done what?' Jess pressed.

'Goddammit—done whatever you're crawling on us for!'

'Could've been some of the Box K boys,' Red suggested, trying to be of help to the floundering Zurcher.

Holloway gave them a taut smile. 'That's what you'd like for me to believe—only I know better.'

'How—' Red began, and then hushed instantly as Walt Zurcher flashed him a warning look.

'Not important how,' Jess said, the same tight grin on his lips. 'You made your try and it didn't work. Next time something happens I'll look you up and it won't be to talk.'

'You ain't scaring me off,' Zurcher said. 'Man's got a right to do his own choosing.'

'Going to be risky for you. I'll stand for no

more trouble.'

'You blaming me for this ruckus between the Morrels and the Lindseys?'

'Not for starting it—for keeping it going and making it worse.'

Zurcher shrugged. 'Better be telling Dave Morrel to move on, too.'

'I'll handle him my way. Right now I'm talking to you.'

'And maybe I ain't listening so good.'

'Up to you. I aim to keep things from getting any worse around here—and you're the spark that could set it off.'

Walt picked up his cards, toyed with them. 'You sound like some tin-star marshal. How much time you giving us, Mister Lawman?'

Holloway clung to his temper. 'Day's young. Just keep remembering that it'll be you who'll do the dying.'

The outlaw stiffened. 'Maybe,' he said quietly.

Jess nodded curtly and wheeled around. Eyes on the mirror of the back bar, he crossed to the doors, closely followed by Gurney.

Reaching the batwings, he paused. Neither Zurcher nor any of the others at the table, aware of his surveillance, had stirred.

'That's the way it will be from here on,' he said over his shoulder. 'I'll be watching every move you make!'

CHAPTER TWELVE

Holloway stepped out onto the gallery of the Mulehead, stopped. Art Gurney moved up beside him. The old puncher was silent, disappointed in the encounter; he had expected a showdown—a killing, Jess realized, and now was having his doubts. He faced the grizzled oldster.

'Not the way you figured I'd handle it?'

Gurney wagged his head. 'Speaking plain—it ain't. You ought've called Zurcher out, settled things with him once and for all. Was what Saul would have wanted.'

'Maybe. Right now killing's not the answer here.'

'Be a few who'll say you backed down . . . '

'Their privilege,' Jess said, disinterestedly. 'Always a lot of people anxious for a fight—long as they're not in it.'

Art made no comment, only stared off into the street. Inside the saloon Walt Zurcher laughed.

'Reckon he figures he come out on top,' Gurney said. 'And he'll be telling every man that walks through them doors so.'

'Let him,' Holloway snapped. 'He knows better. Don't aim to turn a family squabble into a first class range war unless I'm forced to. I'm heading out to see Lindsey—talk—'

'No call to make the ride,' the old puncher said, pointing toward the far end of the settlement. 'That's him and his missus coming now.'

Jess swung about. The rancher and his wife, in a light buggy, were slanting for Gholson's. He remained motionless until Lindsey had pulled up to the rack in front of the store, then stepped off into the dust and crossed over.

He touched the brim of his hat in a courteous greeting to the woman, nodded to Lindsey. 'Was on my way over to talk with you.'

The rancher, in the act of wrapping the reins about the whipstock, did not look up. 'Don't know as we've got anything to chaw on.'

'Wrong there. If we don't get a few things settled pretty quick, it'll be too late.'

Lindsey stiffened. 'That a threat?'

'No. More like a promise. Things keep piling up way they are, someday we're going to have a mighty bad explosion.'

'What did you want to talk about, Mr. Holloway,' the rancher's wife asked, leaning forward.

Lindsey jerked around, gave her a sharp look. She only smiled, continued to study Jess.

'The cattle drive. Did some asking, found

out how all this trouble got started.'

'Wasn't Box K that got it going!' Tom Lindsey broke in angrily.

'Doesn't matter now who it was. Thing to do is call a halt.'

'Just like that, eh?' Lindsey said, snapping his fingers. 'You're a fool, Holloway, if you think a little jabbering's going to wipe out all the—'

'Don't expect it to,' Jess cut in, 'but I expect you to be man enough to try and end it. And you're smart enough to know it'll come to bloodshed one of these days.'

The rancher's jaw tightened. 'When it does, I reckon we can take care of ourselves.'

'Point I'm getting at . . . No call for it to go that far.'

'Up to you—the Morrels.'

A short, balding man wearing a bib apron appeared in the doorway of the store, leaned against the frame. Gholson, apparently, taking it all in.

'What was it you wanted to say about the drive?' Mrs. Lindsey prompted.

Instantly the rancher whirled on her. 'Stay out of this, Hannah!'

Hannah Lindsey squared her shoulders, thrust her chin forward. 'I won't stay out of it! Lot of foolishness—every bit of it. Go ahead, Mr. Holloway.'

'I figure we ought to throw the herds together, make one drive to Springer.'

'What was that?' Lindsey demanded in an incredulous voice.

'Seems there's always been trouble over trail grass. First herd across never leaves much for the one that follows. And there's been some meanness mixed up in it, too.'

'Like burning it off—'

Jess nodded. 'There's plenty of grass for all if it's handled right.'

'And you figure running the two herds together'll fix all that?'

'It will. Be no more of this first man there gets the gravy—second man gets the leftovers, thing. That's been the bone of contention—at the bottom of everything.'

Tom Lindsey stared at Holloway, smiled. 'Now, you wouldn't've hatched out this little scheme after you found out my herd's ready to move and Morrel's ain't, would you?'

Jess shook his head. 'Didn't know where you stood—and I think the Slash M beef is ready, or just about.'

The rancher studied the backs of his hands. After a moment he shrugged. 'It's some kind of a trick—'

'No trick. And I'm not asking you to turn your stock over to me or anything like that. We'll each run our own crews, take separate chuckwagons if you say. And we'll both go along. Be just like any drive except we'll move out together.'

Again Lindsey was silent for a time. Then,

'Heard you'd fired them hardcases that's been hanging around Morrels. That true?'

'It's true. They've been warned to move on.'

'Don't mean they will.'

Holloway stirred, dismissed the statement. 'What about it? You agreeable to make the drive together?'

'You talk this over with the Morrels?' Lindsey countered, his eyes reaching beyond Holloway.

Jess said, 'Not necessary. Except they'll see it my way, however.'

'Now's a good time to find out,' Lindsey replied. 'Here comes Dave.'

Holloway turned, watched Morrel head in toward the rack fronting the Mulehead. He noticed then that several men had gathered on the saloon's porch, were listening to the discussion taking place between Lindsey and himself. In the forefront were Walt Zurcher and Red. Elsewhere he could see Nemo and the two strangers who had been at the table.

Dave dismounted, wrapped his reins around the pole. Zurcher stepped up to him spoke briefly and fell back. Immediately Morrel wheeled, crossed the street and confronted Holloway.

'What's this talk about making a drive with Lindsey?'

'What I plan to do if he's agreeable.'

'The hell you will!' Dave snapped. 'Time'll

never come when you'll see Slash M stock walking with Box K stuff!'

'It's here now,' Jess said calmly. 'Now go on over and play with your friends. This is none of your business.'

Dave Morrel flushed hotly. 'My stock—by God, I got a right—'

'You gave up your rights when you started running with Walt Zurcher,' Holloway said. 'Move on!'

Tom Lindsey laughed. Dave threw him a furious glance, spun on his heel and returned to where Zurcher and the others stood. Not pausing, he mounted the step and entered the saloon. After a moment, the outlaw, trailed by his friends, followed. Jess waited until all were inside and then, raw with impatience, weary of the endless bickering, turned to the rancher.

'What about it? Let's get this settled.'

Lindsey rubbed at his chin. 'Got to do some studying. Ain't so sure—'

'Well, I am!' Hannah Lindsey declared in a firm voice. 'This thing has gone far enough. I want it stopped—and it seems to me Mr. Holloway has the right idea!'

'Now—wait a minute—' Lindsey began.

'No—you wait. Marie Morrel and I were friends for a long time but this argument between you and Saul broke it up—and friends and neighbors aren't so plentiful that you can spare even one! Besides—as he said—it's going to end up in bloodshed if we don't stop it. What do you want us to do, Mr. Holloway?'

'Call me Jess for one thing, Ma'am,' Holloway said, breaking the tension. 'Then next I reckon we ought to decide on a place to gather the herds.'

'Crater Canyon be the best,' Art Gurney, silent through it all, suggested. 'You think so, Tom?'

'Be the best,' the rancher said slowly. 'When?'

Jess glanced at Gurney. The old puncher spat. 'Slash M stuff's ready—or almost. Figure was we to start pushing hard today we could be in the canyon tomorrow. Drive could begin next morning.'

'That'll be Saturday. Move out at sun-up.' Jess said. He stepped forward, extended his hand to Lindsey. 'Be nobody sorry for this. You've got my word.'

The rancher nodded. 'Probably something we should've thought of years ago. But I reckon I'd never got around to believing it if this here wife of mine hadn't done some pushing.'

Jess smiled at Hannah Lindsey, expressing his gratitude, and wheeled to cross to the roan. He had a glimpse of Red moving through the batwings of the Mulehead, going into the saloon—knew immediately what it meant.

Dave, or Walt Zurcher, had sent him back to listen, to see if Lindsey would agree to the proposal. They would know now that he had. They would be aware, too, of the location of the gather and the hour of the drive's beginning.

CHAPTER THIRTEEN

'Trouble brewing sure'n hell,' Gurney muttered, eyes on the saloon doors. 'Knowed you should've cut Walt Zurcher's water off right when you had the chance.'

Jess slanted a look at the old puncher. 'Only a dead man's a good man, that it?'

'Depends. If you're talking about the likes of Zurcher and his bunch, I'm agreeing.'

Holloway was silent for a few moments. 'You ever kill a man?'

Gurney hawked, spat. 'Can't say as I have—'

'Didn't think so. Makes a big difference,' Jess said and moved on to where the roan gelding waited.

They mounted, headed north out of the settlement for Morrel's. Holloway was feeling better about the situation—thanks to Hannah Lindsey. While there had been a strong possibility Tom would have eventually given his approval of the plan, she had forced him to make an immediate decision. And the drive, if successful, would be a long stride toward peace.

'You still aim to keep this from Marie?' Gurney asked as they broke from the last of the houses and veered west into the cedar studded hills.

'Not much chance of that now. Dave'll break his neck to tell her.'

Art grunted. 'Can bet on it. He sure was put out—Lindsey laughing at him way he did.'

'It was rough on him.'

'Had it coming. About time Dave started doing and thinking right. Take a few hard jolts like that to make him see it. You figure Marie'll try to stop the drive?'

'She's got as much to gain as the Lindseys.'

'But supposing she bows her neck?'

'I'll give her the same choice as I did when I ran off Zurcher. Either I'm the foreman—or she fires me.'

The old puncher chuckled. 'Sort of got her there. She promised Saul she'd let you take care of things. She ain't one to go back on her word.'

Gurney paused, looked over his shoulder. The road had reached the beginning of the higher, brush-covered hills, was beginning to wind its way toward a distant line of ragged buttes. Jess glanced at the older man.

'Something bothering you?'

'Got myself an uneasy feeling,' Gurney replied, shrugging. 'Figure we ain't heard the last of Zurcher and his bunch yet.'

'Not much they can do but talk Dave into trying to stop the drive—through his ma.'

'They could put a bullet in your head,' Gurney said flatly. 'You don't know them skunks like I do.'

'I'll be keeping my eye—'

'I knowed it!' the old puncher said suddenly. 'We're being trailed!'

Jess turned quickly. He caught a fleeting glimpse of several riders in the distance. All seemed to be hugging the edge of the trail as though trying to keep out of sight.

'Don't slow down,' he said. 'Let them think we don't know they're there. You figure it's Zurcher?'

'Who else? Ain't likely to find pilgrims on this road.'

It could be Walt Zurcher—Zurcher and Dave with Nemo and Red and possibly also the two strangers he had seen in the saloon. Jess gave the reason for their pursuit careful thought.

They could have only one thought in mind-prevent him and Art Gurney from reaching the ranch and getting the drive underway. Success—and the healing of the breach between the two ranches—depended on getting Slash M cattle to Crater Canyon on time and being ready to begin the drive.

Lindsey would consider a failure to do so as an indication that the truce was over.

Dave and Zurcher would again have everything their way and the simmering trouble would resume its climb to an inevitable, bloody explosion.

He looked back over the long slope. He could see none of the riders at the moment as brush hid them from view. Abruptly he swung off the trail and cut in behind squat pinon trees. Gurney wheeled in beside him.

'What's up?'

'Got to know for sure it's Zurcher.'

'It's him,' the old puncher said with conviction.

Holloway made no answer, began to angle across the slope for a shoulder of rock jutting from the hillside. If it proved to be someone else, all well and good; they could continue on their way to the Slash M and get preparations started for the drive. But if it were the outlaws—and Dave Morrel—he would have to take steps to head them off, turn them back.

Reaching the bulging fault, he dismounted and moved to its extreme edge. Searching the slope below, he finally located the trail, fixed his gaze upon an open stretch lying between two clumps of brush. The riders would be fairly close—dangerously so—when they crossed the opening, but Jess Holloway felt he had to know for certain the identities of the men.

The moments dragged, became minutes. Art Gurney stirred restlessly. 'Ought to be moving. Going to push us plenty getting the herd to the canyon on time. Chuckwagon's got to be loaded. Remuda lined up—all the boys told.'

'Five minutes won't make any difference,' Jess said. 'Thing we've got to know is whether we can expect trouble from Zurcher or not.'

Gurney bobbed his head. 'Just figure on it. Walt and Dave'll cook up plenty.'

Jeff straightened. Two men had ridden into the cleared area. Their horses were moving at a fast walk while they held themselves high on the saddle, stared up-slope. A moment later three others came into view a bit to their left, another appeared on the right.

'Zurcher and Dave, sure enough,' Jess murmured, his eyes on the two men in the lead. 'Got Red and Nemo—and that pair we saw in the saloon, with them.'

'Six. Regular little army,' Gurney said. 'Walt sure's aiming to just take over.'

Holloway crossed to the roan and went to the saddle. He knew now what to expect—trouble in plentiful quantities! 'How many men can we spare for the drive?' he asked.

'Six, eight . . . '

'Six, including you, ought to be enough,'

Jess said. 'Don't want to strip the ranch. Listen close, Art. Head for the Slash M. Get there fast without letting Zurcher or any of his bunch see you. Pick the riders you want and have them get the herd moving toward the canyon. I'm leaving it up to you to get everything set.'

Gurney nodded, frowned. 'What'll you be doing?'

'Waiting for Zurcher. Got to keep him busy.'

The lines in the old puncher's face deepened. 'What good'll that do?'

'If I can keep that bunch tied down for the day, you won't have any problems getting the stock to the canyon in time.'

Gurney nodded as understanding came to him. 'For a fact! You're the bait that draws off the wolves whilst I move the stock.' He sobered. 'Ain't so sure that's smart. They's six of them to your one—'

'I can handle them. Main thing is for you to get the herd there and ready to head out Saturday morning with Lindsey.'

'What'll I tell Marie?'

'Nothing. Don't let her know what you're up to.'

'Maybe she'll get wise anyway.'

'Then tell her to see me. Say you've got your orders and you're carrying them out.'

Gurney started to wheel away, checked himself. His features were serious. 'Watch yourself, son. Don't go taking no big chances.'

'Never was much hand at that,' Jess assured him. 'Just you see we're ready for that drive!'

CHAPTER FOURTEEN

Holloway waited until Art Gurney had disappeared into the brush and then doubled back to the trail. Walt Zurcher and his men would be near, he realized, and he was cutting matters a bit thin, but it had to be done.

Reaching the roadway he pulled into its center, halted, taking care to not look down-slope; he was gambling on still being beyond pistol range of the outlaws.

From the tail of his eye he saw distant motion. It was only a flash as one of the riders moved into view and then instantly dodged behind some brush. Jess grinned tightly and turned up the trail. The bait, as Gurney had termed him, had been offered.

He rode at a set pace designed to give the old puncher as great a lead as possible while not allowing Zurcher to pull in too close. He looked ahead. The bluffs were no more than a half mile distant. He would make a stand there, he decided, well up in the rocks where he could have a good sweep of the slope below.

He reached the first outcrop of loose shale and boulders. The trail veered left and he cut away, pointing directly toward a deep slash in the face of the nearest butte that would permit him to gain the crest. The roan began to blow as the footing became more difficult. Drawing his rifle, Jess dismounted, moved out, leading the gelding.

They reached the ravine, narrow and filled with feathery Apache plume and sharp-pointed yucca. They started the climb. The roan snorted and heaved as the shale and storm-washed gravel skidded from under his hoofs, but he managed to stay upright. Finally they reached a narrow level and halted.

Holloway glanced around. They were just below the summit, now within easy reach. He could see Zurcher and the others, absently counted them—six men. They still followed the main trail, apparently unaware yet that he had veered off. That was good. It was important the outlaws think he and Gurney were still together and headed for the Slash M.

Leaning the rifle against a rock, Jess led the roan the balance of the way to the crest, stationed him out of sight in a hollow below the rim, and then returned to the ledge. Taking up the long gun, he checked the magazine, assured himself that it was full and laid it upon a flat slab of sandstone at the end of the shelf. Drawing his pistol, he retraced his steps and took up a position at the opposite point. That done, he settled down to wait. He was ready . . .

Dave Morrel and Zurcher came into view first. They rode side by side on the trail, both craning their necks as they looked ahead. Their horses now moved at a faster gait indicating that the rough area of the buttes had evidently been selected as the place where they intended to close in on the two men they thought were still in front of them.

A few lengths to the left the four other men, now in a single group, made their appearance. They were abreast, and Red seemed to be holding their attention with something he was telling—a story perhaps, or a joke.

Holloway cocked his pistol, and hunched low, moved to the front of the rocky shelf. The range was too great for a handgun, but he was less interested at the moment in hitting one of them than he was in bringing the party to a halt. Taking general aim at Zurcher, he thumbed two quick shots.

Whirling quickly, and still low, he ran to the far end of the ledge, seized the rifle and levered another shot at the remaining men.

Raising his head he looked to see what the effect had been. Zurcher and Morrel had dismounted and sought safety behind a pile of boulders to the right of the trail. Red and the others were also off their saddles and were legging it for a brush-chocked arroyo a half a dozen strides below them. Jess snapped a second bullet at them to speed them on their way. The distance was not too far for the rifle and dust spurted about their heels.

Satisfied that he had made his presence known and established the belief that both he and Gurney were entrenched in the higher rocks of the slope, Holloway returned to his original position. He had them neatly pinned down. The next move was up to them . . .

It was not long in coming.

Red leaped suddenly from the ravine in which he and the three others had taken refuge, sprinted awkwardly across the uneven ground for the rocks where Dave and Walt Zurcher lay. Jess snapped a shot at him with his sixgun, then hurried to the rifle.

Instantly the men below opened up. They could not see him, he knew, and were angrily returning his fire in a burst of exasperation. All were using pistols, having left their rifles on the horses. Holloway turned his attention to that bit of neglected business; it would be stupid to allow the outlaws to improve their predicament in any way.

Aiming at the earth in front of the horses, now clustered in a small circle, he levered three hurried shots. The animals reared in fright, wheeled, galloped off down the slope for a considerable distance. The long guns were now well beyond the outlaws' reach.

A fresh burst of shooting erupted in the wake of this, but the bullets all fell short, thudding into the loose gravel and rocks below the ledge. Holloway continued to peer over the edge; it would be smart to impress Zurcher and his followers even more, of the fact that they were thoroughly covered.

Again it was the redhead.

Jess saw him burst from behind the rocks that shielded Dave Morrel and Zurcher, start for the ravine. Holloway permitted him to get halfway, then, taking careful aim, placed a bullet at his feet.

Red yelled, stumbled, went sprawling full length into the dirt. He gathered himself instantly, began to crawl frantically for the wash. Wasting no more of the rifle's cartridges, Jess threw a revolver shot at the man—more for the benefit of sound than anything else.

With Red again in the arroyo and out of sight, Holloway settled back. He glanced at the sun. It was well onto noon, and cupped in the rocks as he was, the heat was beginning to make itself felt. He thought of his canteen, swore softly at his shortsightedness; it was on his saddle and to obtain it he would have to expose himself. While there was no danger from the weapons of the men below he was reluctant to reveal his exact position.

The day wore on. Thirst began to plague him insistently and he again cursed himself for his neglect. It was the one error in a perfectly executed plan. But he refused to let discomfort bother him too much. There had been occasions when he had gone longer without water, and survived. He had only to wait until darkness fell.

Around three o'clock Dave Morrel made a try for the horses. Jess drove him back with two closely placed shots. As the young rancher dived headlong into the protection of the rocks, the other men began to fire. Holloway sat back, grinned at their futile efforts. He could imagine their fury!

An hour later the shooting, for no apparent reason that he could tell, broke out again. Suspicious, he changed positions, his eyes probing the brush below the rocks where Morrel and Zurcher lay, and along the wash in which the others had taken cover. He could see no movement.

Gravel rattled hollowly off to his left. He wheeled swiftly, threw his glance along the steep face of the bluff. He could see no one, but a small puff of dust was hanging lazily at the foot of the grade.

Instantly he crossed to the end of the ledge, eyes on the welter of loose rock and brushy growth at the base of the butte. A stone clicked—Jess strained to place the slight noise. It seemed to have come from higher up on the bluff—almost parallel to his position.

Abruptly a gun roared, shattering the hush. Dust showered Holloway as the bullet dug into the sun-baked wall behind him. He ducked low, hurriedly tried to locate the marksman.

A second shot came. He saw the bulge of blue-white smoke, the hasty withdrawal of a man's arm as he jerked back behind a jutting of rock farther along the face of the butte.

He realized what had happened. He had figured the arroyo in which Red and the others lay ended when it reached the foot of the formation; instead it probably carved its way to the right, possibly connected with a second ravine. By following it out and making use of distractions afforded by his companions, one of the party had managed to climb the bluff.

Grim, Holloway pulled back, placing the vertical ridge between himself and the outlaw. He looked down-slope, immediately threw his rifle to his shoulder. Zurcher and Dave had taken advantage of the unguarded moments, had left the pile of rocks and reached the horses. As he lowered the weapon, aware of the distance, he saw them mount, draw their own rifles from the boot.

He glanced again at the sun. Too early to pull out—Art Gurney would need until dark. He would have to continue stalling Walt

Zurcher and his men. But he could not do it there—not with one man on the face of the butte who could get in a lucky shot. And now Dave and Zurcher had rifles. If he remained he could become trapped, pinned down.

Whirling, he ducked low and raced up the narrow opening in the rocks for the crest. Bullets screamed against the hard surfaces around him, screamed off into space as Morrel and Zurcher bought their guns into use. He plunged on, gained the top and flung himself over the rim. Not hesitating, he ran to where the roan was picketed, jerked the reins loose and vaulted onto the saddle. Spinning the blue about, he headed for a place on the rim of the butte beyond where he figured the one outlaw was stationed.

He came out barely fifty feet below the man. He was one of the pair that had been in the saloon. Dropping from the saddle, Jess made his way to the edge of the butte. He could see Red, Nemo and the third man. They were below, standing upright in the arroyo, their eyes on the ledge where he had been. Farther over, Morrel and Walt Zurcher, again on foot, were advancing slowly up the grade, rifles poised. Apparently they thought him to still be in the rocks. On the face of the bluff. Steadying himself, he took close aim at the rocks just above the man's head. He pressed off a shot. Dust and rock chips eruted around the outlaw's head.

He yelled, jerked away. His feet lost their perch and he fell, dropping a short distance to the slope and then sliding and rolling the remainder of the way to the bottom.

At the report of Holloway's rifle, Morrel and Zurcher spun. Instantly both began to shoot. With dirt spurting about his boots, Jess hurried to the roan, again leaped to the saddle and whirled away.

Daring their bullets, he kept himself in full view. He had to keep them at his heels . . .

CHAPTER FIFTEEN

He could hear Red shouting about the horses, the words only partly reaching him between the echoing gunshots. The level surface of the rim fell away into a deep swale. The roan dipped over the edge, fighting to retain his footing, and they dropped below the reach of the outlaw's bullets.

Jess pulled to a halt. Dismounting, he went to his belly and crawled to the edge. Morrel and Zurcher, astride their horses, were moving up fast along the foot of the buttes. Their intentions were clear; they hoped to cut him off farther on.

Beyond them, Red and Nemo, their mounts recovered, were swinging to the saddle. One of the strangers was assisting the other onto his horse. Apparently he had been injured in the fall from the bluff. As Jess watched he turned, headed back in the direction of town while his friend hurried to catch up with Red and Nemo, now spurring to overtake Zurcher and Morrel.

Satisfied, Holloway returned to the roan and mounted. He stared ahead, wondering as to the nature of the country. It appeared to be a continuing roll of low, brush-covered hills and smaller buttes. Touching the gelding with his spurs, he moved on.

He would lead them north, playing a grim game of hide and seek in the rough badland until sunset. Then he would shake them off and double back to the Slash M. By that hour it would be too late for the outlaws to carry out their plans.

He crossed before them a short time after that, offering himself as a fleeting target to the five men. All were moving now in a compact group.

They opened up on him immediately. He gave them two answering shots and spurred on, pointing for a low, brush-filled swale a half mile distant. He reached the edge of the hollow, paused to look back. Zurcher, followed closely by Red, Nemo and the tall newcomer, were pulling out of the valley, streaming across a narrow flat.

Where was Dave Morrel?

That question set up a quick worry within

him as he sent the roan loping toward the brush. Had he deserted the party, turned for the ranch?

He shrugged away all thoughts of young Morrel. It was Zurcher and his crowd that presented the greater danger; best he concentrate on them. Later he would meet and handle any problem Dave might create.

His appearance at the edge of the brushy swale immediately brought a flurry of gunshots, most of which fell considerably short. Drawing his rifle, he scattered the men with two bullets, and then plunged into the tangle of rank growth.

At once he was lost to view, as was his sight of them. He swung right, began to cut back toward the buttes. A half mile later a rise lifted before him and he struck for it. Halting on the summit, he looked for the outlaws. They were almost directly below him, and having missed his turn off, were moving straight on.

He remained there finding time at last to satisfy his thirst from his canteen. When the outlaws were finally lost to him in the undergrowth, he came about, retraced his path, intending to get below them. If his hunch were right, Zurcher, not finding him before them, would cut back to the buttes where he could get a better view of the surrounding land.

Jess moved on, allowing the blue to pick

his way in and out of the scrub cedars and thick rabbitbrush. He glanced again to the sun. It was lowering fast. It wouldn't be necessary to maintain the game much longer.

Abruptly the dry scrape of leather against brush, the grunt of a horse, came to him. He pulled up sharp, alarm racing through him. Before he could wheel away, the rider broke into view only paces to his right.

It was Nemo! The gunman's eyes flared with surprise. His hand darted toward the pistol on his hip. Holloway drew fast, fired without aiming. Nemo's mount reared at the sound, shied off.

From somewhere behind the dark gunman, shouts went up. Anger at his own carelessness ripped through Jess. He had been so cocksure of what Zurcher would do—and he had blundered straight into them.

He whirled the roan about, snapping a second bullet at Nemo, another into the general direction of the shouting, and spurred the gelding into a reckless gallop for the buttes.

'Head him off!'

It was Walt Zurcher's voice coming from the left.

'He's making for the bluffs!'

He recognized Red's tones, bent lower over the roan's arched neck. They were close—too close. He looked about, tried to choose a denser area into which he might flee. It was not there. The nearer he drew to the cliffs the more sparse the growth became.

Holloway reacted from instinct. He turned the blue hard right, cut sharp into the last of the thick underbrush. He spurred the horse cruelly, taking his chances on him stumbling, for a good ten yards, then hauled him to a quick stop.

Drawing his pistol, he punched out the empty cartridges, reloaded—and waited. If the outlaws missed his turn, they would continue on toward the crest and he would have no use for the weapon. If they had not been fooled—he would have to shoot it out.

He heard them a moment later, their horses moving at a fast walk. Zurcher's voice was sharp, angry.

'Keep strung out. He ain't going no place, once he gets to the top. We'll box him, in.'

'Could make a run—either direction,' Red said.

'What do you want—somebody holding him for you?'

'Just saying it'll be no cinch—'

'Will be if you're watching what you're doing. We'd a had him right now if Nemo hadn't been half asleep.'

'Goddammed horse,' the gunman muttered. 'Started pitchin'. Couldn't get off a shot.'

Zurcher made some reply but the words were lost to Holloway as the riders passed on.

He slid his weapon into the holster, sighed and swung around. There was no need to bother any longer with Walt Zurcher and his crew; by the time they discovered that he was not trapped against the bluffs, it would be dark.

He cut across the low hills, taking the precaution to remain in the brush, until he was again on the mesa above the ledge where he had made his stand. He crossed over, made a junction with the trail and curved west.

With the shadows lengthening and growing darker around him, he put the gelding to a comfortable lope and headed for the Slash M.

Everything should be ready by that hour—or nearly so, he felt, and failing as he had, Walt Zurcher would likely give it up. The drive should get underway with no problems. He wondered if Dave had been able to stir up any amount of trouble for Gurney. Decided that such was unlikely. Matters would have been too far along for him to prove a hindrance.

He topped a hill, saw the lights of the ranch glowing through the darkness far below. He realized then how tired he was—and hungry. He'd check with Art Gurney as soon as he rode in, assure himself that all was in readiness; then he would have a bite of supper and pile into bed. He wanted to be in good shape when the drive began.

He passed under the gate heading, pulled the gelding to a walk. No use arousing Marie Morrel. It would just mean an argument—and he was too beat for that.

Reaching the main house, he circled by it, moved on to his quarters. A shadow detached itself from the blackness along the bunkhouse. In the pale moonlight he recognized Dave. A pistol glinted in the boy's hand.

'Climb down!' Morrel ordered, grasping the roan's head-stall. 'You're calling off the cattle drive.'

CHAPTER SIXTEEN

Jess Holloway made no move to comply. Slumped on the saddle, he studied Morrel's taut, angry face. Apparently he had figured it right; Dave had arrived too late to do anything about the herd—was now playing his last, desperate card.

'Forget it,' he said quietly. 'Drive heads out in the morning . . .'

'Hell it does!' Dave shouted, waving the pistol threateningly. 'I'm giving you an order—and you're taking it!'

Holloway shook his head. 'I don't take orders from you—gun or no gun. Might as well put it away.'

Fury overwhelmed Dave Morrel. He lunged, seized Jess by the arm, attempting to drag him from the saddle. Holloway slipped sideways, caught the horn as he came off. He kicked free of the stirrups, struck hard on one heel. Instantly Morrel crowded against him, clubbing with his pistol. Jess took a glancing blow on the side of the head. There was little pain but it sent his own anger soaring.

He caught Dave by the wrist, spun him half around, slammed a knotted fist into his belly. The younger man gasped, struck out wildly. Holloway ducked the blow, slapped Morrel hard across the face. Dave staggered back, dropped his revolver. Holloway, thoroughly aroused, kicked it off into the darkness, shoved Morrel against the bunkhouse wall, started another blow.

'That will be enough!'

Marie Morrel's sharp, precisely pronounced words cut the half darkness like a knife. Holloway stepped back, chest heaving, turned to face her.

She stepped to Morrel's side. He sagged against the building, head slung forward, one hand pressed to his middle as he fought to recover his wind.

'Dave—are you all right?' she asked, touching his shoulder.

He jerked away savagely. 'Leave me be!'

Marie frowned, stared at him for a moment, and shifted her attention to

Holloway. 'What's this all about?'

Jess shrugged. 'Little misunderstanding.'

'Misunderstanding—hell!' Dave grated. 'Ask him what he's doing with our cattle.'

'The cattle?' she echoed. 'What about them?'

'Better question would be to ask him what he's been doing all day,' Jess replied coolly.

Marie shook her head impatiently. 'I don't know what's going on here, but I intend to find out. And I don't want questions—I want answers. You, Holloway, what about the herd?'

'He's throwing it in with Lindsey's—that's what!' Dave said before Jess could reply.

'Throwing in? What's that mean?'

'Means instead of fighting with him over trail grass and maybe running ten pounds of meat off every steer we've got, we'll move the stock out together in one big herd.'

Marie Morrel's eyes opened with surprise, filled quickly with hostility. 'You'd dare do that without my permission?' she demanded in a low voice.

'Figured there was no point in asking—you'd be dead set against it, so I went ahead. Cattle's in Crater Canyon right now, with Lindsey's stock, waiting for daylight.'

'What makes you think you can trust Tom Lindsey?'

'He trusts me—and that's good enough far

as I'm concerned. Anyway—what difference it make? I'll be there, using our own drovers. Lindsey'll have his—and the cattle sure won't mind walking together—'

'It won't work, Ma!' Dave broke in. 'You know that. Lindsey's got some kind of a trick up his sleeve. Only reason he agreed—'

'Lindsey will live up to his bargain if we stand by ours,' Holloway said. 'Reason I had to keep you and your friends pinned down in the buttes today. Couldn't let you interfere . . .'

Marie turned to Dave. 'Pinned down?' she repeated questioningly.

'He held a rifle on us—'

'Us?'

'Walt—and Red and Nemo, couple others.'

'Tell it straight—or I will,' Jess said, a note of warning in his tone. 'I figure she'd like to know why you wanted to stop Art Gurney and me—with bullets—so we couldn't get the herd to Crater Canyon in time to meet Lindsey.'

'You tell her,' Dave snapped. 'You've got a good start.'

'Go ahead,' Marie said, looking at Jess. 'I think I'd rather hear it from you.'

'Not much else. We saw them following us, after we'd set the deal up with Lindsey. I sent Gurney on to get things started while I kept Dave and his friends busy. Had to get the Slash M stock to the canyon in time or

Lindsey'd figure we'd changed our minds—and then we'd be right back with the same old problems—worse maybe.'

Marie Morrel was quiet for a full minute. Finally she looked at Holloway. 'You think moving the herds together will—will end the trouble?'

'Step in the right direction. Shouldn't be too hard to iron out whatever else is causing the quarrel.'

She nodded. 'I guess it's worth any risk—'

'Not in my book!' Dave exploded abruptly, stepping away from the wall. He leaned over, scooped up his pistol and jammed it into his holster. 'I won't have nothing to do with it—and you're a fool if you do, Ma!'

Wheeling, he headed toward the main house, walking in quick, angry steps. Moments later hoof beats sounded through the hush.

Marie remained silent until the drumming had faded entirely and then she faced Jess. 'Your idea—and it better work,' she said curtly, and turned away.

Jess grinned to himself, watched her leave. She knew he was right and was giving him her stamp of approval. In those moments she reminded him of Saul—of his way of doing things.

He heard the door slam when she entered the house, and sighing, took up the trailing leathers of the roan and led him to the barn.

Turning the weary horse over to a sleepy stable boy, he doubled back to his quarters, and stepped inside. A figure sprawled on the bed, snoring deeply.

Jess lit the lamp, looked closer. It was Gurney. The old man sat up, scrubbing at his chin, and gazed about in astonishment.

'Dark—by dang! Must've dropped off whilst I was waiting for you. Just ride in?'

Holloway nodded. The old puncher appeared to be all in; the day's work had been almost too much for him. 'Everything ready?'

Gurney yawned, pulled himself to the edge of the bed. 'Ready—and waiting. Chuckwagon, remuda—the whole shebang.'

'How many riders on nighthawk?'

'Six. How'd you make out?'

Gurney wagged his head. 'Kept myself clear of the ranch. Didn't want to go bumping into Marie—or him either. Why?'

'Had a few words with them when I got in,' Jess said, sinking onto the chair. 'Everything's all right with her.'

'She's agreeing to the drive with Lindsey?' the old man asked, surprised.

'She is. But not Dave. He just took off in a big hurry for town.'

'Reckon you know what that means.'

Jess nodded, drew his pistol and checked its loads. 'All our men armed?'

'Expect so. Usually are.'

'Better be sure before we pull out.'

Gurney got to his feet. 'You figure Dave and Zurcher'll try stopping the herd?'

Holloway looked up slowly. 'I'm sure of only one thing—we've got to make this deal work.'

CHAPTER SEVENTEEN

The morning was gray, and cool with a hint of rain to come as Jess Holloway, sided by Gurney, rode into Crater Canyon. The herd, a vast, dark mass strung out in a thick line along its floor, was beginning to stir. Here and there small fires marked the positions of the riders who had spent the night with the cattle, and the two chuckwagons, drawn up at widely separated points, showed signs of life as the cooks began to prepare the early meal.

'Us—over to the left,' Gurney said, pointing off into the faint, smoky haze.

Jess said, 'Meet you there,' and swung to the opposite direction.

He circled the near edge of the herd, noting all were Box K brand, and the thought came to him that the strict isolation of the two ranches was still in effect. It wouldn't hold for long; once the cattle began to move they would mingle. Perhaps then some of the tension he could feel as he rode toward the Lindsey camp would fade.

The rancher squatting back against the front wheel of the chuckwagon, and nursing a tin cup filled with coffee, glanced up as Holloway swung in and stopped. His face was pinched and drawn, and the early morning sourness of a man too old for the job lay upon him like a blanket.

Jess nodded, said, 'Guess we're all set.'

Lindsey grunted, motioned indefinitely at the coffee pot suspended above the fire. 'Help yourself.'

Holloway stepped down. The cook tossed him a cup with total indifference. He caught it, crossed to where the blackened container hung, and under the cool eyes of two Box K riders eating breakfast, poured himself a measure of the steaming liquid.

He grinned at them, returned to where Lindsey sat and hunkered down close-by. 'Looks like a fine day coming,' he said, attempting to break through the wall of hostility.

Lindsey nodded shortly. 'Hope so. Keep your boys in line, Holloway. Been one scrap already. I won't stand for no hoorawin!'

'I'll look after them,' Jess said, faintly angered by the rancher's attitude. 'But the sooner you and your hands get that chip off your shoulders—'

'Right where it belongs,' Lindsey cut in. 'Just you see that Slash M bunch don't try knocking it off.'

Anger again stirred Holloway. If you believed Tom Lindsey, it was always the Morrel riders at fault, never a Box K man. Perhaps it was true, considering Dave and Zurcher—but it wasn't reasonable to think Slash M was always in the wrong. He let it pass. No sense in getting off on the wrong foot.

Finishing his coffee, he rose. 'Obliged,' he said, putting the cup aside. 'We'll be ready to move soon as the men eat.'

'Better be pretty quick,' Lindsey observed. 'We're about to get under way.'

Holloway stiffened. He was doing his best to hold his temper but Lindsey was pushing hard. 'You don't start until I give the signal,' he said coldly.

The rancher's face darkened. 'Now—wait a damn minute—'

'No—you wait!' Jess snapped. 'Deal we made was that the herds move together. If you have to hold up a few minutes for me—you'll do it. Be the same if you aren't ready—we'll wait. And we stay in one bunch. Won't hurt the cattle to mix—they're all branded.'

Lindsey dropped his gaze. After a moment he said, 'What's the signal—a gunshot?'

Holloway turned to the roan, mounted. 'I'll send Art Gurney with word,' he said and pulled away.

He found all of the Slash M punchers at the

wagon having breakfast. Accepting a plate from the cook, he moved to where he faced them.

'One thing I want straight with you here and now,' he said claiming their attention. 'There'll be no trouble on this drive between you and Lindsey's riders.'

'They look for it—they'll get it,' a squat, balding man said drily.

'Not while we're on the trail,' Jess snapped. 'When it's over you can do as you damn well please. That clear?'

'We just supposed to set back and let 'em spit in our eye—that it?'

'They won't—long as you mind your own business. Now get finished. Time we're moving.'

He turned, and beginning to eat, walked slowly toward the cattle. The herd was up, milling around restlessly. Gurney fell in beside him.

'What'd I tell you? Going to be like setting on a keg of gunpowder.'

'Not if I can stop it. First man to start something will find himself out of a job—on the spot.'

'Little rough, ain't it—nailing our boys?'

'Same goes for Lindsey's men. I'll see to it.' Holloway paused, 'You through eating?'

'Reckon I am . . .'

'Ride over and tell Lindsey we're ready to go. I'll get the boys on the saddle.'

The old puncher ambled off. Holloway, having a second thought, called to him. 'Tell Lindsey to take the point.'

Gurney nodded, continued on toward the picket line. Placing the rancher at the head of the herd away from the dust, was only right. The older man would be spared the hard, disagreeable work punchers taking the swing, or side positions, and those at drag, the rear of the cattle, would undergo. Tom Lindsey wasn't as young as he used to be.

An hour later the stock was on the way, flowing out across a broad plain, pointing for the not too distant mouth of the valley where before there had been trouble over the grass.

Jess, circling the herd, checked position of his riders, as well as those of the Box K men, found everything to his liking and forged to the front. Lindsey, on a chunky little black, was well out in the lead. That he was pleased—and relieved—to be riding point was obvious, but he made no mention of it when Holloway swung in beside him.

'Figure to cut straight down the middle of the valley,' he said, pointing ahead. 'That'll let the cattle spread out, graze along the slopes both sides.'

Jess nodded. 'Leaving it up to you.'

'Ought to reach Rocky Point by dark.'

'Eighteen mile or so. All easy going.'

Jess grinned, said, 'Be fine. You lead the way. I'll see the herd keeps up.'

He dropped back, noting the Box K chuckwagon and its trailing remuda off to the side. Morrel's equipment and spare horses were on the far, opposite side of the drive. He shook his head wearily. Maybe, before the trip was over, he could get the two cooks to join forces, establish a common camp.

Three steers darted abruptly from the herd directly ahead of him. A Box K rider yelled, surged forward to haze them back into line. Immediately the steers split-two going one way, the third another. Jess jerked off his hat, swung the roan after the single as Lindsey's man turned to cut off the pair.

Holloway got his runaway back into the mainstream, swerved to give the puncher a hand. Together they drove the two strays into the bawling cavalcade. He started to move on, glanced at the Box K man wiping dust from his eyes. 'Contrary critters!' he shouted.

Lindsey's man grinned, bobbed his head, and Jess rode on.

He saw Ed Floyd a few minutes later, and caught a quick glimpse of the vaquero, Gonzales. Neither man saw him, however, and he did not swing from his path to interrupt them.

The herd was staying together well and giving the riders little trouble. Such was due partly to the coolness of the weather, Jess realized, and partly because the drive was young. The cattle were rested, in good condition, and not in need of water. Their tempers could change in another day. He hoped the drovers would have changed, too, if such proved to be the fact. A hard to manage herd and a crew of hostile, sore-head punchers was a combination he did not care to think about.

A light shower fell late in the morning, but it was insufficient to settle the churning dust. By noon a close humidity had set in and man and beast alike were absorbing punishment. It was of short duration, however. As they approached the rock edged, narrow mouth to the valley, a strong breeze sprang up and immediately the heat was broken.

Jess, riding with Art Gurney, pulled off to one side, watched as the herd slimmed down, and following Lindsey, began to funnel into the valley.

'Doin' better'n I figured,' Gurney said, biting off a corner of his tobacco plug. 'Was plumb sure something would've happened by now—couple of the boys tangling, or maybe Dave and Zurcher trying a cute stunt.'

'Still a long way to go,' Holloway replied, thinking not of the crew but of Morrel and his friends. 'Can't see them letting things slide—not after the way Dave acted last night.'

A spatter of gunshots, coming from the valley, sounded above the noise of the herd. Jess threw a quick look at Gurney. The old puncher's jaw was grim.

'Counting our chicks too soon,' he said.

Holloway wheeled fast, jammed spurs to the blue and rushed for the entrance to the valley. Guns were continuing to crackle, and as he dropped off the plain into the broad swale, he saw a dozen or more steers sprawled dead in the dust. The rest of the herd was milling uncertainly, beginning to split into smaller bunches and scatter.

Jess slowed, glanced hurriedly around for signs of the bushwhackers. Through the haze he saw four riders on ahead. There seemed to be more hiding in the rocks along the slopes. At that moment Lindsey, doubled over on his saddle, one hand clamped to his side, appeared through the dust. Ed Floyd was with him. The rancher saw Jess, slanted toward him.

'This why you wanted me out front?' he asked in a dragging voice. 'So's I'd be an easy target?'

CHAPTER EIGHTEEN

Anger roared through Jess Holloway. 'Don't be a damn fool!' he snarled.

Fresh shooting broke out somewhere to their left. Holloway tried to see through the drifting clouds of dust, could determine nothing. He drew his rifle, faced the men.

'Art-get Lindsey over to the chuckwagon so's he can get fixed up. Ed—I'm leaving the herd to you. Keep the cattle circling—don't want a stampede on our hands.'

'Where you going?' Lindsey demanded.

'Out there,' Jess said, pointing in the direction of the gunshots, and spurred away.

'You can't fight them alone—' Gurney yelled after him. There were other words but they were lost in the bawling din of the confused herd.

He rode on, keeping to the fringe of the heaving, darting cattle, eyes sweeping back and forth as he sought to locate the attackers. There were at least two dozen steers down. He saw a rider stretched out on the grass, a broad stain covering his chest. It took only a glance to know that he was dead.

A bitter fury gripped Holloway. This was the work of Dave Morrel—of Zurcher; this was their way of showing him, and all others, that they were in control along the Cimarron. He shook his head. He could understand the workings of Zurcher's mind, and those he had apparently hired to aid in the attack—but Dave Morrel? It was difficult to believe that the son of his old friend Saul could be a party to such a senseless thing.

A rider raced in from the slope to Holloway's right, emptied his revolver into a small jag of steers loping for the hills. Jess brought up his rifle, took quick aim at the man and fired.

He saw the outlaw wheel and stare at him in surprise, his features unfamiliar, and then suddenly fold and tumble from his saddle.

Immediately Jess cut away, started for the rocks on the hillside. More shooting was coming from that point. He saw a steady run of smoke lifting from behind a clump of cedars, hurriedly poured two shots into the dense shrubbery. The smoke puffs ceased. Moments later a rider burst into the open and started down the grade at a reckless gallop.

Holloway snapped a bullet at him, saw it spurt sand on beyond the laboring horse. The outlaw was too far for a second try. Yells were rising back on the level ground and he wheeled about. Floyd, with three riders, was moving in on the cattle, trying to circle them. Likely the Box K foreman had other men on the opposite side working toward the same purpose but the dust was so thick he could not be sure.

Jess turned, came off the slope, thinking it best to stay in front of the cattle. He caught sight of two riders curving in toward Ed Floyd and the punchers helping him. Riding ahead, he kept his eyes on the pair; it was impossible to tell if they were outlaws or more of the crew coming to assist the herd.

A moment later he recognized Red. The man with him was another stranger. Instantly

Jess slid his rifle into its scabbard, drew his pistol, and sent the roan rushing toward the pair.

'Red!' he shouted, slicing in between the cattle and the two men.

The redhead fired without pausing to aim, apparently recognizing Holloway's voice. Jess squeezed off his shot, saw Red jolt, fall heavily from his horse. He swung to the other outlaw, now veering off. Holloway took close aim at the hunched figure, released his shot. The man straightened suddenly, clawed at his saddlehorn, and raced on.

The riders rushed up to him, came to a sliding halt. Gurney! With him were Gonzales, the vaquero, and another Box K man.

'Figured you oughtn't be by yourself!' the old puncher shouted.

Jess nodded. 'Keep ahead of the herd. Careful who you're shooting at. Dust makes it hard to tell.'

'How many out there?' Gurney asked.

'Don't know. Three, maybe four. Zurcher and Nemo for sure.'

Gonzales leaned forward, cocked his head. 'Also Dave Morrel, eh?'

Jess shrugged. 'Could be.' He was still finding it difficult to accept.

'If Walt Zurcher's running things, you can bet on it,' the Box K puncher said.

Holloway made no comment, simply rode

away from the others. They moved in behind him and he waved them aside.

'Spread out. Keep your eyes peeled.'

He doubted if Zurcher had given up yet—the outlaw would inflict as much damage as possible, hope to impress upon all the depth of his ruthlessness. If possible he would stall the drive completely, scatter the cattle. In so doing he would not only prove his point personally, but uphold Dave Morrel's position.

He reached the outer edge of the dust pall, looked around. The slopes of the valley were quite near but he could see no movement among the rocks and brush. Gurney and the others had disappeared and he started to double back when gunshots sounded behind and to his left.

Instantly he wheeled, plunged into the floating curtain of yellow particles. Dimly he could see riders cutting through the cattle but he could not tell if they were drovers or not.

He drew closer, saw Art Gurney, rope in hand, lashing at a small bunch of steers, trying to turn them. Other punchers beyond him were doing the same. Jeff pushed on, reaching the outer, ragged edge of the herd, furious at his inability to locate the source of the shots—and therefore the outlaws. The sound had been close, or seemed so, but in the swirling noise and confusion, it was difficult to tell.

The gunshots erupted again—hard to his right. He whirled, saw Gonzales and the other Box K man bearing straight for a knot of riders coming from the center of the herd. His nerves tightened. Zurcher and Nemo! He rode ahead, hurried to catch up with Lindsey's men.

Zurcher saw the oncoming riders. The party split, three of them curving to one side, Walt and the little gunman to the other. Holloway grinned wolfishly. Their choice had been to his liking—they were moving toward him.

He veered the roan left in order to meet them head on. The blue was suddenly deep in the herd, fighting to hold his footing among the crowding, shifting steers. It was a dangerous place to be, but Holloway was so engrossed in facing the outlaws that he gave it no thought.

Shooting over to the right told him Gonzales and his partner had come to grips with the rest of Zurcher's crew. He saw Nemo turn, look to that direction, and in that same moment notice him. The gunman shouted something at Zurcher and both men began to turn away, lashing their horses mercilessly as they sought to force a path through the cattle.

Holloway cursed, fearful of losing the pair in the crush. He brought up his pistol to fire, lowered it. There were drovers on beyond the two outlaws. Sawing at the reins, he got the blue turned, felt him tremble as he breasted a solid wall of steers.

Anxiously, Jess began to shout, lash out at the cattle as he tried to help the roan. He could barely see Zurcher and Nemo through the haze—and then abruptly he felt the gelding going down under him. He tried to leap clear, but he was hemmed in on all sides.

Holstering his pistol, he jerked off his hat, and still astride the blue, began to slap at the long heads of the steers closing in around him. The blue was fighting to get back on his feet. He made it, partly went down again as a longhorn crowded against him.

Jess became aware of shouting, and then of Art Gurney and another rider fighting their way toward him. He lashed out again with his hat, grateful for the fact the cattle were so jammed they scarcely moved.

'Hi'yuh! Hi'yuh! Hi'yuh-h-h-h! Dang jugheads!'

Gurney's rasping voice was close. Jess got himself clear of the blue, stood to one side. Taking the headstall in his hand, he urged the horse to rise. The roan began to struggle again, and then as Gurney and his helper came in, hazing the stock across to create a small island, he pulled himself upright.

Holloway leaped onto the saddle, turned his eyes to the direction where he had last seen Zurcher and Nemo. There was no sign of them. He sat back, swore deeply. He became aware of Gurney's hoarse voice.

'What in tarnation you doing here—middle of the herd? Aiming to get yourself tromped?'

'Zurcher!' Jess yelled back. 'Him and Nemo. About had them when my horse went down.'

The old puncher raised himself in his stirrups, glanced around. 'Where'd they go?'

Jess shook his head. The puncher with Gurney said, 'Was four riders lining out across the slope for town few minutes ago.'

Holloway came to attention. That would be Walt and Nemo—and what was left of his bunch. Zurcher had pulled out, convinced he had accomplished his purpose, that he was still master south of the Cimarron.

But Walt Zurcher was wrong, Jess thought grimly; and if there was to be peace he would have to be driven from the country. Holloway recalled his earlier decision to avoid violence, to not create bloodshed. It was too late for that now. There were dead men in the valley; Tom Lindsey and possibly others had been wounded. Zurcher—and Dave Morrel—had laid down the challenge. It was up to him—to accept it—not in vengeance but as a means for bringing it all to an end.

Holloway swung the roan about, started for the slope.

'You going after them?' Gurney yelled.

Jess nodded. 'Get the herd moving for

Springer. I'll be back.'

CHAPTER NINETEEN

He rode into Willow Creek knowing he was expected. Zurcher would have planned it that way.

Halting in front of the clapboard church at the end of the street, he looked ahead. The walks were deserted and there were no horses at any of the hitchracks. Checking his pistol, he moved on, pointing for the general store. Zurcher and Nemo would be in the saloon, directly opposite.

Pulling up at Gholson's, he dismounted, keeping the blue between the saloon and himself, and looped the reins around the bar. He paused then, probed the empty doorways and quiet shadows along the roadway, saw no one, but the hushed tension told him he was not alone, that the entire town was there watching—waiting.

He stepped from behind the blue, crossed to the saloon's porch in deliberate strides. Approaching the swinging doors from an angle, he stopped, peered into the dark interior. He could see the dim figure of the bartender, of a lone patron sitting at a table.

He let out a long breath, settled back on his heels. If Zurcher and the others were inside, they were back, out of his line of vision. Moving fast, he lunged through the batwings, whirled to face the hidden corner. There was no one there. Turning, he came back around, intending to question the bartender. His glance fell upon the lone customer. It was Morrel.

Anger whipped through Holloway. He crossed to the table. 'Where is he?'

Dave raised his head. 'If you're talking about Zurcher—I don't know.'

'Little hard to believe.'

Morrel shrugged, twirled his empty glass between his fingers. 'Suit yourself. Fact is, haven't seen him all day.'

'Hard to believe that, too,' Jess said in a low voice. 'Next thing you'll be telling me you don't know he jumped the herd, shot up Tom Lindsey and some others—slaughtered a lot of good beef.'

Morrel was silent. He reached for the bottle before him, poured himself a drink. 'No, didn't know that. Tom bad hurt?'

'He'll live.'

'Glad to hear it,' Dave said, swallowing his liquor.

Jess smiled tightly. 'I'll bet . . . You going to tell me where I can find Walt and Nemo?'

Morrel shook his head, 'It's the truth—I don't know.'

Holloway wheeled impatiently, threw his hard, pushing glance to the bartender.

The aproned man shrugged. 'Ain't here. All I know.'

Jess Holloway came full around, strode to the doors and stepped out onto the porch. He could have been wrong; Zurcher and his crowd may not have returned to town—could possibly have read the signs correctly and kept going. But that didn't sound like Walt Zurcher.

He had Dave Morrel tucked inside his pocket, had a good thing going—and with only one man standing between him and what he wanted—he'd not walk away now. No, Walt Zurcher would be around somewhere.

Jess eased off the porch and into the street, his eyes narrowed to shut down the sun's glare as he searched along the buildings. Near the center of the dusty roadway he came to a halt. Motion in the shadows just within the livery doorway caught his attention.

Imperceptibly, he settled himself squarely on his feet. A faint coolness began to blow through him as his hand dropped to the pistol at his hip. A man emerged from the stable's entrance, started forward slowly. Holloway's muscles tensed . . . Nemo!

A second figure stepped into view, leaving the passageway just this side of the bakery. He was a tall, stooped man wearing two low slung weapons. He was one of those who had taken part in the raid; Holloway recognized the ragged Stetson he had pushed to the back of his head.

And then Zurcher . . .

Jess watched the outlaw walk into view from still a different point along the street, a fixed smile on his lips. They had set it up this way, placing him between them, he realized, thus making it impossible for him to face them all. Zurcher had stacked the odds.

Silent, he allowed them to approach. They were taking their time, hoping, perhaps, to shatter his nerve, force him to go for his gun without thinking and place himself in their cross-fire. He wouldn't play it that way. He'd wait—concentrate on Walt Zurcher; his death counted the most. If he still stood after that, he'd try to get off a shot at Nemo before he was cut down. He had no choice except to ignore the tall gunman, whoever he was.

Holloway heard a sound behind him, saw Zurcher and Nemo come to a stop. Dave Morrel's voice broke the warm hush that lay over the street.

'Reckon you could use some help.'

Surprise rippled through Jess. Not removing his eyes from the three outlaws, he said, 'You're standing on the wrong side.'

'Not any more,' Morrel replied moving up to Holloway's shoulder. 'Done a lot of thinking. Guess I acted like a kid last night. Other times, too. But I grew up fast. Want me taking a hand in this?'

'Up to you.'

Zurcher and the others had resumed their slow, indolent advance. Jess said, 'Don't understand this. You didn't know about that raid?'

'No. Something Walt cooked up on his own. Haven't seen him since yesterday—when you tied us down on the buttes.'

'Glad to hear that. Drive's going on through. Things'll be all right around here now. Lindsey's convinced.'

'Same as me—and Ma,' Dave murmured, added, 'getting close enough. Who you want?'

It sounded like Saul Morrel speaking. Holloway grinned, said, 'I can handle Zurcher and Nemo. You take care of the tall one.'

'When?'

'Soon as they reach the front of the harness shop—'

At that instant Nemo broke for his weapon. Jess drew fast, thumbed a shot at the man, whirled to face Zurcher. He heard Dave's gun blast twice as he turned, heard it again as he drove a bullet into Walt Zurcher and sent the outlaw staggering back, clawing at his chest.

He hung there, half bent, silent, as smoke coils floated around his head. And then, as tension broke and sweat began to glisten on his face, his taut shape relented. He turned to Morrel, saw him resting on one knee, clutching at a blood soaked spot on his thigh.

'That tall one—he was fast,' Dave said with a wry grin. 'But he was a mite low and wide.'

Holloway dropped beside him, began to examine the injury. 'Like your pa used to tell me, being fast was good—'

'But being accurate was better,' Dave finished. 'Must've heard that a thousand times!'

Jess laughed, glanced down the street to the bodies of the outlaws. 'We had us a good teacher,' he said, getting up. He pointed to Morrel's leg. 'Flesh wound. Not bad.'

He turned, faced the people now rushing into the open. Several had gathered around the outlaws. Others were hurrying toward him and Dave. He beckoned to a couple of the nearest.

'Give him a hand to Doc's,' he said.

The two men crowded up, helped Dave to his feet. Morrel pulled away from them. 'Where are you going?'

'Back to the valley. Got that drive to finish.'

'Hell—I can ride. I ought to be along.'

Holloway shook his head. 'Wait 'til next year. Way it looks now, I figure you'll be taking over right soon,' he said, and smiling, crossed to the waiting roan.

Photoset, printed and bound in Great Britain by
REDWOOD BURN LIMITED, Trowbridge, Wiltshire

95-6 cir
0016 cir
106-25 cir

GB 98

JUNIATA COUNTY LIBRARY, INC
498 JEFFERSON STREET
MIFFLINTOWN, PA. 17059